About the Author.

Ian Colquhoun is an author and actor o
now resides in Edinburgh. This book
first being his autobiography 'Burnt: ?
man's inspiring story of his survival after losing his legs' which was
released on Mirage publishing in 2007. Ian lost his legs following a vicious
unprovoked assault and arson attack whilst he was living in the Irish
republic in 2002, an attack that saw him receive no compensation
whatsoever. Prior to losing his legs he worked as a warehouse operative.
He has appeared as himself on TV's 'Men in white' in 2006 and on
'Richard and Judy' in August 2007, as well as starring in 'Ocean of fear', a
film about the sinking of the USS Indianapolis during World War Two
(2007). Ian has also appeared in SMG's long running police drama
'Taggart'.

A keen historian, Ian's particular areas of expertise are the Jacobite
wars in Scotland and Ireland and the conflicts of the 19th and 20th
centuries.

He can be contacted through either of his websites.

www.iancolquhoun.org.uk or www.myspace.com/ian0478

DRUMMOSSIE MOOR

JACK CAMERON, THE IRISH BRIGADE AND THE BATTLE OF CULLODEN.

Ian Colquhoun

Published 2008 by arima publishing

ISBN 978 1 84549 281 6

© Ian Colquhoun 2008

Printed and bound in the United Kingdom

Typeset in Garamond 11

Swirl is an imprint of arima publishing.

arima publishing
ASK House, Northgate Avenue
Bury St Edmunds, Suffolk IP32 6BB
t: (+44) 01284 700321

www.arimapublishing.com

All interior artwork is by Martin Symmers of Edinburgh.

This book is dedicated to the memory of all Scottish and Irish soldiers who have fought and died in a multitude of foreign armies over the centuries and to those who chose resistance at home instead. You will never be forgotten.

About this book

Firstly, I hope you enjoy this new approach to writing history. In my 20 years as a historian I've rarely found anything that bridges the gap between serious academic history and the mass appeal of historical fiction. I have tried to bridge that gap with this work by combining a fantastic story with accurate research. It is my dearest wish to see this work turned into a screenplay for TV or film later down the line. I hope you get as much enjoyment out of reading it as I did out of researching and writing it. You are essentially getting a gripping story, some stunning original artwork and an easy to use glossary to explain certain aspects of the Jacobite wars in more depth. Enjoy!

Acknowledgments.

I would like to thank the following people for all their help, encouragement, constructive criticism and downright inspiration over the last 5 years and for giving me the self-belief to write this novel.

Thanks to my brilliant artist Martin Symmers.

My family, Davie 'Disco' McDermott, Martin 'Bumpmates' O'Donnell, Jenny Hood, John Norton, Maggie McDermott, Tony 'mad-dog' Divers, Chris Brown PhD, Stuart McHardy MA, Dr Sharon Adams MA, Lynn Nelson, Robert Hogg, Mikey Williamson, Samantha McAfferty, Mark Oakes, Olivia Giles, Steve Richards, Amputees in action, Alana, Hibeesbounce and anyone else who has helped me since the dark days of 2002/2003.

In memory of my Uncle and Godfather Ian Merrilees and my Auntie Mauren Colquhoun Trotman. RIP

I make no apologies for the pro Jacobite nature of this book.

PRELUDE

It was the eleventh of May 1745. Over one hundred thousand men faced each other in an area of no more than a few square miles. Fifty thousand men of a Catholic Franco- Irish army faced fifty thousand men of "The Pragmatic army", a mix of German, British, Dutch and Austrian troops. This was the *War of the Austrian succession* at its height.

The huge Franco-Irish army was besieging the Flanders town of Tournai, which was defended by some seven thousand Dutch regulars who hoped to be relieved by their allies sooner rather than later.

Knowing that a relief force of some fifty thousand men was on its way to attempt to break the siege, the legendary French commander, *Marshall Maurice de Saxe*, had laid an elaborate trap for the approaching 'Pragmatic army'.

With a river holding their left flank and some dense woods protecting their right, the French army was arrayed on top of a low ridge that ran at a right angle to the small, insignificant Flanders town of Fontenoy.

On either side of the town the French had constructed a series of fortifications and redoubts that, along with the river and the woods, would hopefully funnel the advancing allies into a clear area between Fontenoy and the trees. If the plan worked, the Allied army would be destroyed by concentrated French musketry and artillery fire before they could form an effective firing line of their own.

The British and German forces were commanded by King George II's second and favourite son, *William Augustus, Duke of Cumberland*, and to Saxe's surprise, his opponent led his army into the dead ground between the woods and the town and straight into the Franco- Irish trap.

Cannonballs thudded into the densely packed ranks of the British redcoats as they plodded forward stolidly. Awaiting them on the crest of the ridge stood the French infantry in line formation ready to engage in the inevitable fire- fight that would decide the battle. A thin line of blue and white coated Frenchmen facing a cumbersome, densely packed column of British redcoats. Theoretically, the French had the advantage being deployed in line as every soldier could fire his musket, whereas only the front few ranks of the British column and a few men on the flanks could fire their weapons.

To the rear of the French line stood several thousand Irish troops dressed in long skirted red coats. A short but well built Lieutenant by the name of O'Neil was checking his troops and shouting encouragement to his men, with the aid of his fearsome looking Irish Sergeant. The red-headed Sergeant barked orders at the men, then, satisfied that they were positioned suitably, took his place to the left of the line beside a pint sized private soldier.

"So O'Donnell, are you ready to give these English bastards some of our Irish steel?" enquired the Sergeant, not taking his eyes from the unfolding battle to the front.

"I don't think we'll get a crack at them Sergeant McDermott sir, our gallant French comrades will blast that column to bits before it even crests the ridge."

"Is there something wrong O'Donnell?" asked the Sergeant, "you haven't moaned or complained about anything all day".

"No sir. I was thinking about me da. He would have been proud to see me today. Proud to see us all actually."

"Well, fix your bayonet and keep looking in front boy" continued the Sergeant "you might yet get a chance to kill some Englishmen."

These two men and the rest of the Irish brigade stood sullenly as the smoke from the cannonade began to obscure the battle only a few hundred yards to their front. They heard the first volleys from the French regulars lining the ridge and then the counter volleys of the British came next. CRASH! CRASH!

After about twenty minutes, thousands of French troops, some wounded, some just plain running away, began to fall back towards the second line and even beyond it into full retreat. What on earth had gone wrong?

Lieutenant O'Neil waved his sword in the air, signaling to the Irish to get ready to fire when the advancing British appeared out of the smoke but, just as he was about to roar his command, a cannonball struck him, taking of his legs. Two soldiers carried the maimed Officer to the rear.

"What now Sergeant?" whispered O'Donnell to Sergeant McDermott.

"We wait," replied McDermott.

Against all odds, Cumberland had led his column directly against the French lines and shattered them like a battering ram. The men in his column couldn't all fire as they were so bunched together but they had nevertheless pushed Saxe's battle hardened regulars back of their ridge. The British were now attacking the redoubts and fortified strong points in turn with relative impunity, storming each position one by one. The French and their Irish allies were losing the battle, and possibly the war.

"That'll be our trip to Scotland to restore the King postponed again then Sergeant" moaned Private O'Donnell. "So much for the whole brigade going to Scotland whilst these English soldiers are busy over here, it'll all be off again I tell ye, at least until we can beat them here".

"Don't speak too soon lad" said McDermott as he left the line to speak to the next company's Officer. Soon the shout came up *"Prest!"* *"Prest!"* and all the men in the Irish brigade charged their bayonets.

"Those English bastards have pushed our French comrades off the ridge, what say we go and chase them back down again, *Cuimnidh ar Luimneach agus ar Feall na Sasanach!"* roared McDermott.

The lads in the ranks shouted back that they were ready and steadily started to advance into the smoke to take on the as yet unbroken British army.

The thick gunpowder smoke stank of rotten eggs and reduced visibility to only a few yards, but the Irish brigade advanced to within about eighty yards of Cumberland's rapidly advancing column.

"Halt!" roared McDermott. "We'll give them one volley then we'll give them some Irish steel".

The British, now drawn up in line opposite their foes, fired the first volley and it took a heavy toll of the Irish but they stood firm. Now it was their turn to fire whilst their British enemies nervously reloaded their muskets. Standard tactics of the day dictated that in battle, opposing lines would exchange volleys until one side had had enough and retired. That was how ordinary soldiers fought in ordinary battles, but this was the Irish brigade.

"FIRE!" roared McDermott and thousands of musket balls tore into the British ranks, decimating the front few rows. As soon as this devastating wall of lead hit Cumberland's troops, the Irish brigade fell upon them with the bayonet, screaming their battle cry" *Cuimnidh ar Luimneach agus ar Feall na Sasanach".*

This unorthodox tactic worked brilliantly and drove the British, who had only minutes before been on the verge of a famous victory, into a retreat that was more like a rout. They simply weren't expecting a ferocious bayonet charge like that in the middle of a fire- fight and took to their heels. They were led from the field by their intrepid commander Cumberland, leaving behind some seven thousand dead and another three thousand prisoners. The Irish had put their French comrades to shame and not for the first time either.

When all was over, the Irish lads tended the wounded as best they could, their own and the enemy's, then marched off to storm the fortifications of Tournai now that its chances of relief had evaporated.

"Well there's a turn up for the books O'Donnell, we won. Looks like we might get sent on our little Scottish adventure after all."

O'Donnell smiled and replied to his Sergeant "We'll restore the King then we'll go back home to Ireland, I was getting a little bored with France anyway. And if these British regiments we routed today are anything to go by we shall have an easy time in Britain when the invasion comes."

Sergeant McDermott didn't reply.

The regiment was sent to the port of Dunkerque to join the massive French army camped along the channel coast. They waited. And waited. And waited. Finally news reached the Irish brigade in July 1745. Volunteers were wanted for an expedition to Britain to restore its rightful monarch and to divert British attention from the main continental struggle. Only eight hundred men were originally assigned to the expedition. There was no shortage of volunteers from the men of the Irish brigade, eager for another crack at the English.

CHAPTER ONE

REDCOATS

The redcoats advanced cautiously towards the highland town of Elgin. Their boots clumped noisily on the crude track and their fixed *bayonets* glinted in the morning sun as they warily approached the seemingly peaceful town.

All seemed quiet ahead as the soldiers marched in loose order, keeping their eyes peeled for any signs of the enemy but at the same time being transfixed by the beautiful highland scenery around them. Lush greenery and purple heather dotted the landscape around them but a cold breeze reminded them that winter had not long passed. A great stag appeared to the left of the tiny column on a steep brae but it was well out of effective musket range so some of the men just gaped at the fearsome yet noble beast in admiration.

The column inched closer to the ancient market town like a thin red snake slithering through the heather. There was not much in the way of activity going on in the usually busy market town ahead, little if any noise could be heard and there were only a few isolated pillars of smoke rising from chimneys dotted around the town. The soldiers marched on.

Their Officer, a tall robustly built man with short brown hair, looked for signs of life ahead and warned his men to be on their guard. He carried a standard *flintlock musket* with fixed bayonet, unusual but not unheard of for an officer, as well as having a fearsome blade at his side.

If intelligence was to be believed there were enemy soldiers nearby and at any moment a volley of musket fire might decimate the advancing redcoats. It mattered little to the tall Officer that their prospective enemies were irregular highland troops, many of whom were primitively armed with broadswords and shields and some even carrying old *matchlock muskets*. This was those 'irregular' troops' native country and his red coated subordinates were mostly newcomers to the Scottish highlands. In the Officer's eyes that evened things up a little, although he still had every confidence in the ability of his experienced redcoats to stand up against anything they might come across.

It was quiet though. Too quiet.

The only sound other than that made by his own troops that the officer could hear was an open door to a nearby house that banged against its frame in the brisk highland breeze.

The redcoats numbered sixty men including their Officer and as they marched down the town's main street towards the dilapidated castle they deployed into a loose skirmishing order so as not to present an easy target for any would be enemy snipers. Where were the town's inhabitants?

Slowly, cautiously, the soldiers reached the town's normally bustling marketplace. There was still no one to be seen anywhere. An eerie silence hung over the town, broken only by the occasional cackle of a crow or the clump of soldiers' boots on the stone track.

The men stopped beside a well in the middle of the deserted market to fill their canteens and their Officer took the standard precaution of posting sentries and sending out two small patrols to try and establish why the town appeared deserted and, more importantly, to ascertain where the reported enemy clansmen might be lying in wait.

The Officer spoke with his Sergeant and drank from his canteen. Both men were experienced soldiers and could smell a trap, the question was, where and when would it come?

They did not have to wait long for their suspicions to be confirmed as, all of a sudden, a ragged musket volley from a row of houses to the left oblique crashed into the red coated company, downing four men. The volley was followed by a blood-curdling roar that heralded the enemy's surprise rush from cover towards their red-coated foes.

The redcoat Officer reacted coolly, having his Sergeant arrange the company in double ranks facing the enemy who were charging wildly across the open market square. The Sergeant had the redcoat front rank kneeling and the rear rank standing behind them. They were soon joined by the sentries and the men of the two patrols.

Around one hundred enemy clansmen bore down on the red-coated line, screaming war cries and waving broadswords. It was a terrifying sight. Desultory pot shots from nearby houses rained in on the redcoat company but the musket fire was poorly directed and mostly sailed harmlessly over the redcoat company's heads. Meanwhile, the ferocious charging highlanders had got to within sixty yards of the redcoats before the tall Officer gave the order for his front rank to fire. Thirty muskets roared, instantly obscuring the red line in a veil of smoke, then another twenty six shots rang out from the second line, making both sides temporarily invisible to one another.

The redcoat Sergeant bellowed the reload command and the men bit off the ball from their paper cartridges, opened and primed their musket's pan, closed the pan, poured the remaining powder and paper down the muzzle, spat in the ball and then forced it home with the ramrod.

"Make ready" roared the Sergeant and fifty-six flints were set to full cock, ready to fire again.

"Hold your fire" interrupted their Officer.

The smoke had cleared revealing twenty to thirty dead or dying tartan clad warriors strewn about the square in front of the company. The remaining highlanders could be seen retreating through the town in obvious disarray and the redcoat Officer saw his opportunity to complete his victory by ordering his company to advance on them.

It soon became clear that several houses had been converted into well-defended strong points and it took a good hour of disciplined well-directed fire as well as painstaking bayonet work from the redcoats to neutralise them before they could continue their advance on Elgin castle.

At the other side of town a group of around twenty enemy highlanders rallied and charged again, catching the redcoats by surprise and closing with them for hand to hand combat. The highlanders were led by a ferocious looking ginger haired man carrying two pistols and a *basket hilted broadsword*. The man's badly scarred face gave him the persona of a possessed warrior demon as he killed two redcoats at point blank range with his pistols before attacking the redcoat Officer with his sword.

The Officer dropped his musket and drew his own blade, easily parrying the crude attacks of his adversary but unable to deliver a decisive blow of his own thanks to the scarred highlander's round shield. Fortunately for the redcoats their numbers began to tell and the ginger haired scarred highlander ordered his men to retreat. The redcoat Sergeant sent twenty men to follow the clansmen while the rest of the men were put to work securing the town and locating its inhabitants. The redcoats had lost six men killed with another five wounded while twenty two enemy highlanders lay dead or dying around them.

It had been an ambush, but not a very professional one, typical of irregular highland troops. The Officer set his men to piling the enemy bodies and collecting their arms and ammunition, though his chief concern was now the fate of the as yet unaccounted for townsfolk. Where were they?

Twenty minutes later, the redcoat detachment sent after the highlanders by the Sergeant returned, informing their Officer that the enemy had fled and was nowhere to be seen.

Shortly afterwards a patrol of red coated cavalry trotted into town, keen to see what all the noise had been about. Their officer, a young Lieutenant, approached the red-coated infantry Officer, dismounted, saluted and then proceeded to relay orders to him.

"Captain Cameron" said the Lieutenant *"Brigadier Stapleton's* compliments, you are to complete your mission and return to the Prince's army at Inverness as soon as time permits". These were no English redcoats.

CHAPTER TWO

WILD GEESE

Captain Jack Cameron was a newly commissioned Officer of the *Irish Brigade* in command of a detachment of *Dillon's* infantry. The Irish Brigade were Irish exiles who fought in the service of France and her allies, and their units and indeed many of their men were descendants of the Jacobite army which left Ireland in 1691 to form the army in exile of the deposed British king *James II and VII* following the *treaty of Limerick*.

James had been deposed in 1688 mainly due to his Catholicism which made him unpopular with many of his English subjects, but his many supporters had come to be known as Jacobites, from the Latin for James, *Jacobus*.

James had been replaced on the British throne by his son-in-law *William of Orange* and his own protestant daughter Mary, following the birth of his own Catholic son, James Edward in 1688.

A failed attempt by James to hold Ireland had ended in defeat in 1691 but the generous peace terms offered by William allowed James' twelve thousand-strong Catholic army to be repatriated to France in what became known as *"the flight of the wild geese"*.

In the decades since, these units, and a few similar Scottish regiments, had served the French Kings in their wars from Spain to India and were among the best units in the French army. There had initially been two Irish armies in French service, the Irish brigade and King James' own army in exile but in 1697 they were amalgamated to form one Irish brigade, and there was no shortage of recruits from Irishmen disillusioned with tyrannical British rule at home who saw serving France as a way to get at England without bringing war and devastation to their own native land.

By 1746 many men of the Irish brigade were French-born though they did have to be of Irish descent, and many of the brigade's original member's sons and grandsons now emulated their ancestors by serving France and the exiled Stuarts. This adherence to the Stuarts was particularly dangerous for men who had enlisted in the Irish brigade from 1745 onwards, as in that year the British government, constantly facing regiments of Scottish and Irish exiles in French service had made joining foreign armies illegal.

The irony of the Irish brigade was that they wore red coats just like their *Williamite* and later *Hanoverian* adversaries, as the Irish brigade originally considered themselves to be the legitimate British army in exile, though their long skirted red coats were different from those worn by the other "redcoats".

This particular unit of the Irish brigade was part of a contingent sent to Scotland by France in late 1745 to aid the rebellion of James II and VII's grandson, *Charles Edward Stuart*, an attempt to regain his family's rightful throne from the *House of Hanover*, who had been given the British crown by the English in 1714, in a bid to secure a protestant dynasty.

There had been three hundred men of the Irish brigade, as well as five hundred men of a Franco-Scottish regiment, the *Royal Ecossaise*, in the Jacobite army and there was also supposed to have been a Franco-Irish cavalry regiment, *Fitz James' horse*, but the ever-vigilant Royal Navy had intercepted all but one squadron of the cavalry en-route to Scotland, as well as all of their horses, meaning that the seventy odd cavalrymen who did get ashore had to be mounted at the expense of Scots horsemen.

Jack Cameron had been made a Captain in Dillon's company at *the battle of Falkirk* three months earlier, upon the untimely death of their own Officer. His military knowledge and experience of both British army and French army life had made him an invaluable addition to the Jacobite army when the rebellion broke out in August 1745.

With the town seemingly secured, Captain Cameron re-formed his men and they set off to discover the fate of the townspeople and complete their mission, which was to secure a substantial store of powder and ammunition that Jacobite intelligence said was hidden in Elgin castle.

Cameron had more than just the general welfare of the townsfolk in mind, he had been in Elgin when the rebellion had started eight months previously, in the company of a young woman, and he had enjoyed that liaison considerably, in fact, he couldn't wait to see her again. Her name was Mary Kerr, the daughter of a local saddler, and she was one of the most beautiful women he had ever seen. Twenty-four years old with long black hair, big brown eyes and ample shapely breasts. She also had the warmest of personalities and the most caring of hearts. Cameron hoped to see her that night as he fancied she would make a fine Mrs Cameron one day. He seemed to get on OK with her father too, which was a bonus, though the old saddler and merchant was a tad nosey regarding

Cameron's army and its intentions. Still, what was to be expected in an area so traditionally Jacobite?

He did not have to wait long to see Mary again. Private O'Donnell discovered most of the townspeople cowering in the church, the doors having been barred from the outside. O'Donnell and two other men had managed to get the doors open, with great difficulty. At first no-one came out of the church, so Cameron and Sergeant McDermott decided to go in and see what was wrong.

To his utter astonishment, Cameron saw Mary. She smiled when she saw him and Cameron realised that she was heavily pregnant. There were only women and children in the church, no men at all, which was odd.

Still, Cameron's heart felt overjoyed at seeing Mary again. He had only left her side some eight months earlier after a whirlwind romance to fulfil his lifetime ambition and join the Jacobite army, but he had promised her he would return when the war was over. Now they threw their arms around each other and shared a long embrace.

"I knew you'd come back, Jack," said Mary in her sweet Scots accent "I knew you wouldn't leave me."

As Cameron looked deeply into her big beautiful eyes he noticed she had bruising around her head and left eye.

"Mary it fills my heart with joy to be with you again and I have dreamt of this moment since we parted but alas it is duty that has brought me here today" said Cameron. "Where are all the town's men? Where are your father and brother?"

At first, Mary said nothing. Looking around the church Cameron noticed Mary wasn't the only one with bruises, most of the women and children had scars and bruises, all of which looked fairly recent. They had obviously been deprived of food or water for the duration of their captivity too, so the soldiers helped out as best they could, sharing oat biscuits and water with them. Mary spoke again.

"They came at dawn yesterday morning, Jack, they took everything of value and they led off all the men, to where we do not know."

"Who?" asked Cameron, "Who came?"

Mary told Cameron that the previous morning, Elgin had been visited by government troops. Around one hundred men of the *Argyle militia* and a troop of English cavalry. The Argyle militia were men of *clan Campbell* who were loyal to the ruling house of Hanover and who despised those with Jacobite sympathies.

They had not only led off the town's men and left the women and children in the church to starve, but they had also made off with everything of value in the town, including all the livestock and produce from the market and a huge cartload of ammunition that had been hidden in the old town castle.

"You're safe now my love" Cameron reassured Mary "and I assume that swollen belly you have is something to do with me?" he added.

Mary smiled and nodded then her head sank as she looked to the ground and started to cry.

"I'm sorry Jack, I fear our child is lost for I have bled all night and have suffered terrible pains." Cameron, stunned, looked again at this beautiful yet bruised woman in front of him. He had often wondered if Mary had been with child in his eight months away from her, the thought pleased him even though they had not been married, in fact, the thought of seeing her again had been of great comfort to him as he got on with his duties in the Jacobite army.

"What happened to you my love?" Mary then told Cameron an astonishing yet chilling tale.

CHAPTER THREE

UNWANTED VISITORS

The first government troops into town the previous morning had been a troop of English cavalry. They had entered the town in an orderly manner and reached the town square where Mary had seen who she thought was Jack leading them in a scarlet coat with a tricorn hat. She had been sure it was Jack. She would have been prepared to swear it.

She had approached, puzzled as to why he was wearing the uniform of the Hanoverians but nevertheless eager to be re-united with her love and share news of her pregnancy, though her huge bump no doubt gave that away anyway.

Instead of a warm embrace and joyful reunion with her lover, Mary got a heavy cavalry boot square in the face which knocked her to the ground. No sooner had she hit the cobbled ground, did she hear the man who was the mirror image of her lover bark orders to his men in a strange accent.

"These dogs have been helping the rebels, round up all the men and lock the women and children in the church, carry away anything of value."

The horsemen were soon joined by the Campbell militia who quickly began to loot the town and herd the women and children into church. Several of the town's younger women were taken to a different house by the Campbells and it had soon became evident from their screams that they were being brutally raped by the Argyle men. Mary had thought that she would be next.

The town's men had been led away eastward by the cavalry and THAT Officer with around ten of the Campbells after they had removed the ammunition from the ruined castle. Command of the town had been left to a fearsome looking red haired Campbell with a badly scarred face and he had carried on rounding up townsfolk. When Mary protested that she was pregnant while being manhandled into the church, the man punched her face with the hilt of his basket hilted broadsword then kicked her forcibly in the belly several times, coldly declaring "silence Jacobite whore, you'll be treated no different with child or without. Nits make lice."

Two of the man's comrades also put the boot into her heavily pregnant belly before locking the church doors, trapping everyone inside.

Mary had spent the night in agony, bleeding heavily and fearing for the life of her unborn child, while her friends tried to comfort her in any way they could until Cameron's men had been able to free them. She had another useful piece of information for her lover, the evil scarred man's name was William Campbell as she had heard the English cavalry officer who looked so like Cameron address him as such.

Cameron initially struggled to take all this in. He had expected to merely complete his mission in Elgin, stay the night with his lover and then return to the army at Inverness the next day. Now he had several problems. Firstly the precious ammunition he and his company had been sent to collect had fallen into enemy hands and secondly, a substantial number of government troops had been in the area when intelligence had earlier said that they were miles away at Aberdeen. He also felt obliged to find out the fate of the town's men folk who had been led east, particularly as Mary's father and brother had been among them.

The bombshell that Mary may have lost their child due to the actions of the English Officer and the brutal William Campbell now gave the mission and it's resolution a personal aspect for him.

What was he to do now? The earlier skirmish with Campbell's men had depleted his company's ammunition to twelve rounds per man while they also had wounded to care for. He also had orders to secure the ammunition supply that the government troops had taken. Should he return to the army empty handed with vague intelligence of enemy movements or remain in Elgin to take care of his wounded and his lover and await reinforcements?

He had fought William Campbell earlier and was confident that next time they met he would kill him. It was Mary's other tale of the English Officer who looked just like him that really had Cameron worried though, and it was news of that Officer that helped him come to a decision. They would neither wait for reinforcements nor return to Inverness, they were going after the ammunition.

CHAPTER FOUR

JACOBITE HEART

Jack Cameron had been born in Edinburgh in 1718, the elder of two twins. His parents ran a busy tavern in the town's *Cannongate*. His father Jack had fought in the two earlier *Jacobite risings* of 1715 and 1719 and his grandfather also had a proud history of fighting for the exiled Stuarts, having fought for King James at *Killiecrankie* in 1689 and alongside the legendary *Patrick Sarsfield* in Ireland, at *the Boyne* in 1690, and again at *Aughrim* a year later. His grandfather had taken passage to France with his family during the flight of the wild geese from Ireland following the end of the Williamite war in 1691. The family was Catholic and pro Stuart through and through. With one exception.

Jack's younger brother, Callum, younger by only a few minutes, had grown up resenting the fact that Jack would inherit the family businesses merely by being a few minutes older. The two had rarely got on. Callum was a butcher by trade and had left the family home in 1737 to seek his fortune in England. He also burned with resentment towards his older brother.

After he had left, Callum had met a girl in Nottingham, the daughter of a local noble. His desire to stay with her and be accepted in his new town had seen him renounce the Roman faith and convert to Anglicanism. The last his family heard he had joined a local militia unit. Jack travelled south in 1738 to attempt a reconciliation with his estranged sibling but by then his brother had changed beyond all recognition. The two men met in a tavern in Nottingham and Callum declared he was going to join the Hanoverian king George's army and that he would not be returning to Edinburgh. Saddened by this, Cameron hung around the tavern for several hours drinking after his brother had left and as a result he was very drunk when the parting shot from his brother arrived in the form of an army *press gang*. Though it was mostly the navy who used the press to swell their ranks, it was not unheard of for the army to resort to forcing men into joining by means of knocking them out cold and carrying them off to a recruiting depot. When the press gang arrived that night Jack had been too drunk to resist and he and several other unfortunate drinkers woke up the next morning as newly enlisted soldiers in the British army.

Jack had lasted a mere four months in King George's army. He completed his training but the iron discipline, monotonously commonplace floggings and the sense of guilt for serving a regime he despised soon compelled him to desert. Now with the threat of the rope hanging over him and being unable to return to Edinburgh in case of recapture, Jack had decided to make for France, where he enlisted in Fitz-James' horse, an Irish cavalry regiment in French service. He served his regiment well, fighting courageously in Flanders on a number of occasions and learning much about military tactics and strategy.

Serving in the Irish brigade gave Cameron enormous pride and he was soon promoted Lieutenant for his gallantry in combat and in recognition of his natural leadership skills.

Jack took a gamble and returned to Edinburgh in May 1743. His parents had died, leaving him the Edinburgh tavern, but rumours of a *Franco-Jacobite invasion of Britain planned for 1744* had also hastened his return to Scotland where he planned to lend his expertise to any Scottish rising which may occur. Life at the tavern alone simply wasn't the same as it had been when his parents and even his treacherous brother had been around and he had soon grown bored of being a landlord. The French invasion of 1744 came to nothing and he was left twiddling his thumbs until the summer of 1745.

That August, rumours had spread that Prince Charles Edward Stuart had landed and raised the Stuart standard, though at first no one knew where. Assuming that he had landed where his father had towards the end of the '15 in the north, Jack headed for Montrose and Peterhead, only to find out that the Prince had landed on the west coast. It had been this seemingly pointless journey north that had seen him stay a few nights in Elgin before heading south to try and join the Jacobite army when it reached Perth. Those three nights in Elgin had of course been where he had met the beautiful Mary Kerr whom he had fallen instantly in love with. He promised to return to her after the war for she was just as smitten as him and the couple looked forward to being married when the rightful king was restored. Now, eight months on, Cameron had returned, to find his love battered and bruised and almost certainly losing their unborn child. He thirsted for revenge.

CHAPTER FIVE

DILEMMA

The news that his brother was nearby and wearing the uniform of King George lay heavy on Cameron's heart. He knew that his brother was probably serving as a Lieutenant in *Kingston's horse*, a volunteer cavalry unit raised in Nottinghamshire specifically for the purpose of crushing the rebellion. He also knew how cold and calculating his brother could be and he worried about the fate of the townsmen who were lead east with him.

Cameron could not, however, let personal feelings get in the way of his military judgement. He consulted his Sergeant and friend David McDermott.

"The army needs that ammo" grumbled McDermott, "and if we can kill those bastards who raided the town and assaulted your good lady then all the better."

Cameron agreed and said "I'll leave you Sergeant along with Private McHardy and any other ten men you choose to look after the townsfolk and the wounded, take cartridges from the dead and wounded and be watchful for those Argyle men should they return."

McDermott nodded and saluted before going off to find his volunteers. Jack embraced Mary and the two shared a deep passionate kiss before saying goodbye once again.

"God speed, my love, and I hope to see you soon" said Mary sadly. Jack smiled and promised her he would return. Mary opened his hand and placed in it a silver brooch she had kept hidden from Campbell and his men.

"Keep this my darling. For luck" she said.

The brooch was shaped like a fish and was extremely beautiful, though Cameron had to be careful not to cut himself on the sharp pin so he put it in his pocket. Although touched by the gesture he had the feeling he would need more than a brooch to complete this particular mission.

The reduced company now numbered around forty men as they formed column and began to march east along the road. It was evening now and the men were tired but they did not complain. Cameron gained a lot of respect from his men by walking rather than riding a horse like other officers, but the truth was, he had little choice anyway, as his horse had been commandeered by the experienced French cavalrymen of Fitz-James' horse. It had been a red coated Lieutenant of Fitz-James' who had brought Cameron the orders that morning to return to Inverness on completing his mission, and Cameron understood why his old crack regiment had been given priority for horses over Scots horsemen, they were simply too good not to be mounted, even if there were only seventy of them.

The men stopped about two miles outside Clashness, a small hamlet on the road east to Aberdeen. Sentries were posted and the rest of the men made camp in a secluded copse of trees beside a stream that gave them ample water. They ate and drank and talked for a while. Cameron had a relaxed but respectful relationship with his new command, unlike the aloofness of British Officers with their own enlisted men. Many of the Irish troops were in Scotland on *furlough*, receiving extended leave from the French army to fight for the Prince and Cameron admired their courage and tenacity. Many of the enlisted men were emulating fathers and grandfathers who had served France and the Stuarts and they dreamed of returning home to Ireland when it was safe to do so with a Stuart monarch on the throne who tolerated their Catholic faith. Cameron admired their optimism.

He had been with the army since it had captured Perth the previous year. He had fought in the first victory over the Hanoverians at *Prestonpans* that September. He had marched through England with the army and seen the bloodless capture of towns like Carlisle, Preston, Wigan and Manchester. He had been sentry outside the *council of war in Derby* that December when the army's leaders debated whether or not to march on London. It was even Cameron who had voiced concerns over the supposed Jacobite credentials of *Dudley Bradstreet*, a mysterious man who had brought news of a huge government army blocking the Jacobites' way to London from Derby, news which tipped the argument in favour of those who wanted to retreat to Scotland to consolidate, and news that had since been found to have been complete fabrication.

Cameron had fought shoulder to shoulder with *McPherson of Cluny's* men in Lord George Murray's brilliant check on the pursuing Hanoverians at *Clifton*, and he had laboured in trenches up to his knees in mud during the pointless *siege of Stirling castle*, a siege that had seen the ranks of the newly arrived Irish brigade and the Franco-Scots regiment,

28

the Royal Ecossaise, thinned by counter fire from the castle and by exposure as the highland troops who made up the backbone of the Jacobite army seemed disinterested in siege work.

Cameron's first glimpse of the Franco-Irish troops had been in the inconclusive battle of Falkirk that January. Though the speedy ferocious *Highland charge* had scattered one wing of the Hanoverian army and put the centre into organised retreat, the charge had been less successful against the other wing where the government troops had stood fast. It had taken a last-gasp intervention from the Irish brigade and the Royal Ecossaise with their well-drilled musketry to finally break the stubborn Hanoverian resistance.

Cameron told his men tales of these exploits and tales of those of his heroic ancestors in Scotland and Ireland while they sat around the fire. Private O'Donnell, drunk as usual, piped up that having had such great successes surely they must win the war soon.

"We beat the English at Fontenoy and we will beat them again" slurred O'Donnell.

Cameron interrupted.

"We have done well lads, but the troops we'll face from now on will be well-led and well-supplied, not like the raw recruits the army routed at Prestonpans and Falkirk I'll wager, nor like the rabble we ourselves chased out of Elgin today. This will be no Fontenoy."

O'Donnell nodded his agreement, things hadn't gone very well since they had defeated the second Hanoverian army sent against them at Falkirk. A disorderly retreat into the highlands after the battle had seen much baggage and artillery abandoned on the way north, due to poor roads. The pointless siege of the highland forts had been a debacle without the abandoned heavily artillery, though they had still taken Ruthven barracks, but this all meant that the main Jacobite army at Inverness was now seriously short on artillery and even shorter on trained gunners. The men hadn't been paid for some time either as *le prince Charles*, the ship carrying vital gold for the Jacobites from France, had never reached Scotland. This meant that the highlanders were now being paid in meal from the last remaining Jacobite meal store in Inverness, a meal store they were now obliged to defend at all costs.

It was well known that the government army of ten thousand men had been training at Aberdeen for some time and that they were well supplied. They were now led by the *Duke of Cumberland*, second son of *King George II* and a man who obviously had a great personal interest in seeing this rebellion crushed.

Cameron realised his talk may dishearten the men a little so he encouraged Private O'Donnell to tell the men a story before they slept while he checked the sentries.

Trudging out towards the most easterly sentry Cameron became aware of voices in the distance. When he reached Private Ross who was guarding the eastward approach, he found the soldier crouched behind a boulder, bayonet fixed, peering into the darkness.

"What have we got then?" asked Cameron.

"Hard to tell sir, I think there's around twenty highlanders, I heard them talking in Gaelic and I made out the silhouette of shields when they crested that hill" answered Ross.

Was this William Campbell come to launch a surprise attack on the sleeping company? If it was he was meddling with the wrong company tonight, thought Cameron.

CHAPTER SIX

A SURPRISE MEETING

Rushing back to camp, Cameron silently woke the men who hadn't long been asleep and led them back to the track where the highlanders were coming from. He had forty men. Twice their number. Silently he deployed the company into three blocks, himself with ten men in line right across their path, while he placed fifteen men on each flank some forty yards away in the heather. The moon was bright and it gave the hills and trees an eerie, haunting, look but it also meant he'd get at least a quick look at the advancing enemy before they saw his own concealed men. The highlanders edged closer. The only sound other than their feet trudging through the heather was an owl that hooted in a nearby tree.

When the approaching highlanders were inside the loose horseshoe formation that Cameron's men had formed, Cameron fired a shot over their heads and roared for his men to make ready. The still of the night disappeared as forty hammers were put at full cock and the obviously shaken highlanders fumbled at their weapons. There was a pause. No one moved. In the moonlight Cameron could see that the highlanders carried French muskets due to the distinctively shaped stock silhouetted in the moonlight. Only Jacobite highlanders carried French muskets.

Cameron called out to the clansmen to identify themselves. They had obviously heard the Irish company cock their muskets and knew they had been taken by surprise. A mystery voice in their midst replied ambiguously that they were "for the King."

Not satisfied with this, Cameron called out "WHICH KING?"

The voice replied "James. God with us."

Cameron realised they were friendly troops and immediately ordered his men to stand down. Approaching the band of clansmen he identified himself and his unit and was in turn told that the men they had nearly blasted to pieces in the dark were a detachment of *Cameron of Lochiel's* regiment, his namesakes. Cameron posted guards on the road and headed back to camp with his newly found allies.

Their leader Alasdair soon informed Jack of what had happened. The Cameron detachment had been sent east to try and locate horses as the army at Inverness had barely one hundred and fifty mounts available to it thanks to a harsh winter, overworking and poor feeding.

The group of thirty Camerons had been attacked late that evening by Argyle militia and English cavalry and had been forced to retire westwards having lost ten men. Only seven had been killed in the fight, the other three captured Camerons including a boy of fifteen had been hanged by the Campbells in the boughs of a tree, apparently on the orders of the English cavalry officer and his scarred subordinate William Campbell. When he spoke of the English cavalry officer, Alasdair stared at Jack, almost in disbelief.

"Am I right in assuming you think you have seen me before?" asked Cameron, guessing that the clansman had already seen the resemblance between himself and the English Officer.

"Aye, you've a brother on the enemy side, a blind man could tell it" answered Alasdair. "That's not an uncommon situation in this war friend" he added.

Cameron explained about the disappearance of Elgin's men and of his brother and Campbell's assault on his heavily pregnant woman, and of his mission to recover the powder and shot.

"Well there are no horses between here and Aberdeen save those ridden by the enemy so I should like to place my kin under your command until we return to Inverness, Captain, and if we can avenge the scum who killed your unborn child, then all the better." Cameron agreed and passed Alasdair a flask of whisky then settled down to grab what sleep he could. Tomorrow would hopefully bring vengeance, answers, and some much-needed ammunition.

CHAPTER SEVEN

DANTE'S INFERNO

By first light the men were up and about, busily buckling on equipment and checking their muskets and ammo. Private O'Donnell sharpened his bayonet against a nearby boulder. Alasdair and Cameron agreed that the highlanders would act as a fast moving advance guard while the Irish company marched in column a little behind them. Cameron now had sixty men at his disposal, around half the number of the Campbell/Cavalry column they were pursuing.

It was a beautiful spring morning. Bird song filled the air from nearby trees, and Private Ross, still exhausted from his nocturnal sentry stint, managed to catch a couple of rabbits that would make a fine alternative to oat biscuits when they stopped to eat. The men passed a babbling burn and stopped to fill their canteens while the hardy highlanders fanned out into the open countryside towards the town of Buckfast.

The column was stopped in its tracks when a black pillar of smoke was spotted coming from the other side of a steep heather covered hill. Alasdair himself led the highlanders towards the source of the smoke while Cameron and the company followed in support, in loose order.

They reached the crest of the hill and looking down saw the remains of what looked like an old barn. It had been set on fire, fairly recently it seemed, though the flames had long since died out. The smoking shell of the barn drew the advance guard of Cameron highlanders towards it. There seemed to be no one else around. Cameron took the usual precaution of sending some of the company out on sentry and left ten men on top of the hill, taking the other twenty down towards the barn. He saw some of his namesake clansmen trying to open the barn door but it had curiously been fastened shut from the outside. One of the highlanders vomited. As Cameron drew closer to the barn he got a whiff of an unmistakable stench he recognised from war on the continent.

Burned flesh!

Finally, they managed to open the barn door and the site they saw was like an image of

Dante's inferno.

A huge pile of charred, unrecognisable smoking corpses lay in the barn. Cameron vomited when he saw this grisly spectacle, as did several of the men. Alasdair was in tears. Around eighty men had obviously been crammed into the barn that was then fastened shut and set ablaze. Looking around it was obvious that no-one had escaped, as no bodies littered the field around the smoking barn. Holding a rag over his mouth, Cameron took a closer look inside. It wasn't easy to tell but it seemed that all the corpses were male. He had found the men of Elgin. This savagery was new to Cameron and indeed to some of his men. They were used to relatively civilised warfare on the continent but this was something new. This had been cold-blooded murder. And Cameron knew it was probably his own brother and William Campbell who had been responsible.

It took the men several hours to bury the charred corpses, no one had the appetite for Ross's rabbits anymore as the men decided to skip eating and get straight after the bastards who had perpetrated this massacre.

Private O'Donnell suddenly shouted for his Officer to come and see something.

Wagon tracks!

The terrain over the last few miles had been steep so they had obviously made up ground on their enemies due to being unencumbered by wagons of their own. The ammunition taken by Campbell and the English cavalry was slowing them down and Cameron's men took heart knowing they might catch up with them soon, even if discovering the wagon tracks confirmed that it was indeed the men of Elgin who had been burnt alive.

Cameron's thoughts turned to his beloved Mary, her father and brother had been in that barn. He vowed to himself that she would not be alone. Jack Cameron was going to have to kill his own brother, and at this rate he was going to enjoy it too.

Cameron ordered the sentries and the ten men whom he had left on the ridge to join them down beside the barn, where they stood beside their clan Cameron allies and offered prayers for the souls of the poor buggars burned alive in the barn. It mattered little that most of the Irish company were Catholic and their highland allies *Episcopalian*, nor that the souls they prayed for were possibly *Presbyterian*. They were united in sadness and grief for their brother Scots and this episode stiffened their resolve to see the perpetrators die.

Cameron knew he had to get back to Elgin for the rest of his men soon and ultimately get back to the main army at Inverness as his superior, Brigadier Stapleton, would want a report on the French units' progress to send back to King Louis at *Versailles*.

There was also the possibility that with the Hanoverians only at Aberdeen, Cameron's small force could either run straight into the full government army moving west to confront the Prince at Inverness or it may not make it back in time to be part of the inevitable battle with the precious ammunition. Time was of the essence now.

The tiny column was soon back on the march. They avoided the main paths and roads, a luxury afforded them by their lack of baggage, and they were soon catching up with Campbell's men. Cameron could smell leather, a sure sign that cavalry had passed by recently and his suspicions were confirmed when they came across a pile of horse dung and a still warm camp fire. Marching on with all speed they came to a vast empty moor with steep sides at the far end and to their left. The place was called Braemuir. There was a stone wall at the far end too and it looked like there was movement ahead. And wagons. Cameron saw his prize in sight. Preparing his sixty-man force for the attack, he initially divided his force in two, with each half comprising an equal split of Cameron clansmen and Irishmen.

Pulling out his telescope Cameron could see there were around thirty of the Campbells concentrated around the wagons. He could even make out the scarred ginger haired William Campbell, the evil man who had fought against him then ran away at Elgin, the man who had kicked his unborn child to death inside Mary. Rage burned inside Jack. He was about to order the advance when Alasdair asked him to speak with him in private. Alasdair was desperate to attack the Campbells with his own men.

"We do this together, my friend," said Cameron "we have come thus far."

Alasdair informed Cameron "the fifteen year old boy hung by them was my son, he was not even bearing arms. I beg you to let us do this."

Cameron saw the rage and hatred in Alasdair's eyes when he spoke of the Campbells and he understood that vengeance was part of the healing process for the clans. He agreed to let the Cameron highlanders perform the attack, but only if he himself could accompany them.

Alasdair answered.

"Bless you Captain, and it shall be an honour to have you with us."
"It will be my honour to charge with my namesake kin." Cameron reassured him.

With no *NCO* or *subaltern*, Cameron was forced to leave Private O'Donnell, the longest serving man, in command of the Irish company while he advanced with the Cameron warriors. As they trudged across the moor, quickening their pace, the Campbells fanned out to form a line in front of the ammunition wagons.

"Remember the barn" roared Alasdair, throwing off his plaid to free his sword arm and drawing his broadsword, his kin following suit. Cameron cocked his musket and ran with them, his sabre bouncing against his thigh. The Camerons let out a fierce Gaelic war cry and broke into a charge, which Cameron, fit as he was, struggled to keep up with. When they got to within eighty yards of the Campbells they were met with a ragged musket volley from the Argyle men, who then dropped their firearms and drew their own swords. The Camerons responded with their own volley, Jack aiming at William Campbell's head. He missed narrowly, the ball ricocheting off a wagon and imbedding itself in another Campbell.

Two Campbells were down but no Camerons were hit and both sides now had empty muskets. It was going to be twenty-eight Campbells against twenty-one Camerons and it would be done with cold steel. This could be a highland battle from four hundred years ago, thought Cameron. Or so he thought. Then he heard a bugle sounding a cavalry charge...

CHAPTER EIGHT

AMBUSH

A seventy man *squadron* of scarlet coated English cavalry came surging over the rise in the ground to the left of the moor. They were almost two hundred yards away but the Cameron's muskets weren't loaded and only Jack had a bayonet, so forming a defensive formation was not an option. The odds were now ninety-eight Hanoverians against twenty-one Jacobites. The Hanoverian cavalry's surprise advance was the signal for the Campbells to advance too and the Camerons were forced to race back across the moor to avoid being caught between the hammer of the Campbells and the anvil of the cavalry.

Their only chance now was to reach the safety of the other end of the moor where the Irish company could provide devastating fire support, but there was still a considerable distance to run. A red coated trooper rode up to Cameron and slashed with his sabre at the Captain but Cameron was an experienced soldier, parrying the blow with his musket before ramming the bayonet into the horse's underbelly. It crashed to the ground neighing in agony and throwing its rider, who barely had time to pick himself up before Cameron slashed his head in two with his sabre. Another cavalryman charged Cameron, firing and missing with his carbine before drawing his sword and bearing down upon the tall red-coated Jacobite, but Jack simply ducked the blow and slashed the trooper across the back, sending him toppling from the saddle screaming in agony.

It wasn't going so well for the other Camerons. Caught in the open they were easy prey for the horsemen, who cut them down mercilessly. Those who did stand to fight were themselves easy prey for the Campbells and their now reloaded muskets. After a few minutes, only Cameron, Alasdair and three other Camerons were still alive, standing back-to-back surrounded by the jubilant Campbells and the hacking sabres of the cavalry. His musket gone, still stuck in a dead horse, Cameron relied on his sabre and alongside his four namesakes, he fought so ferociously that for a brief moment it looked as if they might get away. Then a close range volley of carbine fire from the horsemen felled three of his comrades so that it was only himself and Alasdair left.

The cavalry Captain asked them to surrender, then sent his troopers charging to the other end of the moor to attack Private O'Donnell and the Irish company who had started advancing in an attempt to save their comrades. O'Donnell was no fool and he and the men had faced cavalry before. The logical thing for them to do was to wait until the horsemen were within easy pistol shot then give them a devastating close range volley, but, without their Officer, their volley was delivered too early meaning they had to retreat to the safety of the trees to reload or risk being cut to pieces like their Cameron allies had just been. Cameron and Alasdair were, for the time being, on their own.

The summons to surrender from the English captain did not entice either man to give up, but hearing the Irish company's ill-disciplined weak volley and seeing them with no option but to retreat made up their minds for them. Cameron was technically a French soldier, or at least in French service which theoretically meant he would be treated as a prisoner of war by the British but his namesake, Alasdair, would likely suffer a traitor's death. With a circle of English cavalry around them the two men looked at each other, well aware of what each other's fate would be. Cameron dug the blade of his sabre into the ground, leaving it standing upright before him and took a step backwards, signifying his submission. He considered fighting to the death but the thought of never seeing his darling Mary again persuaded him otherwise, especially when as a French *commissioned officer* he was virtually assured of being exchanged at some point.

"You'll come with us," boomed the English Captain to Cameron, who had his hands tied and was sat upon a horse surrounded by mounted troopers. Cameron looked at the moor, nineteen Cameron corpses dotted the heather of Braemuir along with around nine Campbells and four troopers, it had been a textbook ambush with tactics antedating the *Punic wars* and Cameron, his judgement clouded by anger for Campbell, had fell for it hook line and sinker. Not only that, he had led the brave Camerons into this slaughter and at the same time left his own men leaderless. He was alive though, for the time being anyway.

Alasdair was not so lucky. He was not put on a horse or tied up. Cameron saw the Campbells form a circle around him and give him back his sword. William Campbell was taunting him, the levelled muskets of the other Campbells stopping Alasdair from lunging at him with his broadsword. Cameron could see that William Campbell was a grotesque character, badly scarred with greasy ginger hair and black teeth. He could also tell the man was a psychopath. Campbell ordered his men to aim their muskets away from Alasdair and drew his own sword declaring "I killed that snivelling boy of yours, he danced on the end of a rope and died like a dog" referring to Alasdair's fifteen year old son whom he had earlier hanged. Alasdair, realising the hopelessness of his situation, lunged at Campbell cutting off part of his ear, determined that if he were to die he would take the killer of his son with him.

Cameron was led away by the horsemen, though he saw the rest of the fight. Campbell was indeed a fierce warrior and he and Alasdair fought like demons, though it seemed that Campbell had something up his sleeve. Cameron was elated for a second when Alasdair managed to bundle Campbell to the ground but his heart sank when the other Campbells gunned Alasdair down, just before he could finish their vile leader off.

William Campbell was laughing when he got up.

Poor Alasdair had had no chance, thought Cameron. The vile Campbell had killed the father and son and had probably killed Cameron's unborn child too, as well as the men who had been burned alive in the barn. Cameron swore he would kill him. Though unarmed, captured and tied up under heavy guard, he saw little prospect of that happening in the foreseeable future.

Private O'Donnell was in a state of near panic. He was the senior soldier in the company now but that had little bearing, as they were all Privates. How he wished Cameron or even Sergeant McDermott were there, they would know what to do. With barely enough ammunition left to do anything else Private O'Donnell weighed up their options.

The rest of the men were for going back to Elgin to pick up the Sergeant and his small detachment with all the wounded from the fight there, then going back to Inverness to rejoin the army. It wasn't just ammunition they needed but food and water. At the same time the men felt grief at losing their Officer and their highland comrades and wanted to avenge them, but without leadership and supplies they knew this would be at best optimistic and at worst, suicidal. With heavy hearts and no leader they voted amongst themselves to return to Elgin immediately, it was almost nightfall anyway but they decided to march through the night so they could be there by dawn to give their wounded a better chance of survival. They set off, dumping all their equipment other than their weapons, ammunition, food and water, reluctantly leaving their beloved Cameron to his fate with the English.

CHAPTER NINE

INTO THE LION'S DEN

Cameron only had to ride a short distance with his captors, three miles at the most, until they reached the village of Buckfast. Here Cameron could see what looked like a whole regiment of Cavalry camping for the night. He was bundled off his horse, which was the only offence offered to him thus far by his captors, and taken into a large white tent, the lighting inside of which was very poor. In front of him sat a middle aged man in a scarlet tunic with gold braiding and epaulettes, obviously the regimental commander. The man stared at Cameron for a while indifferently, paused, then spoke.

"You sir, killed four of my troopers today and I see you are the only survivor of your rebel unit." He continued, "You will be taken to Aberdeen and imprisoned until this preposterous rebellion is crushed and its leaders and Officers can face his Majesty's justice."

"I am an Officer in Dillon's regiment in the army of his most Catholic majesty, Louis XV of France, and I demand treatment befitting my rank and status," said Cameron politely but firmly.

The next voice Cameron heard chilled his blood. "My dear brother, so lovely to see you again."

Cameron looked into the shadowy corner of the room, where only one candle flickered, upon hearing the dubious greeting offered by the tent's other occupant. The figure stepped out of the shadows so that Jack could see him properly. Cameron had known it was his brother the instant he had heard him utter his chilling sarcastic greeting.

The two brothers faced each other in the dim light. For both of them it was like looking in a mirror for they looked so alike, being twins. They were of course, both wearing red coats too, Cameron, the long skirted red coat of the Irish brigade, and his brother, the scarlet coat of the Duke of Kingston's light horse. The only difference asides the uniforms was that Jack had not shaved for a few days and had some stubble around his chin, while his brother was clean shaven.

"I wish I could say I'm pleased to see you Callum, but I'm not" was Cameron's reply.

Why did he have to have been taken prisoner by THIS regiment, his brother's regiment, of all the units in the British army?

"And how is that little whore of yours in Elgin, Jack?" was his brother's response.

Cameron thought of asking his brother what he was talking about but he could tell from his brother's tone of voice that he knew exactly what he was talking about. The question was how on earth did he know about Mary? Mary would surely have mentioned if the officer who kicked her or indeed any of the Campbells had asked about the father of her child. Cameron thought it best to stay silent and let his evil brother elaborate on his earlier comment, as he obviously intended to do anyway.

"Oh yes, my dear Jack" continued Callum "We know all about her and the little bastard she'll be having, though hopefully my Campbell friends have relieved you off that particular responsibility."

Jack snapped at this and made a lunge at his brother but he was pulled back by two redcoat guards behind him and beaten to the ground.

"Now now, Jack, temper, temper" gloated Callum smugly, as a sentry's black boot smashed into Jack's face while he lay helpless on the ground.

Jack struggled to his feet and repeated his earlier protest "I am a commissioned Officer in his most Catholic majesty's..."

Callum interrupted "yes, yes, yes, so you said, dear brother" even more coldly and sarcastically.

Callum continued, "I suppose you'll be wanting prisoner of war status, being in the French service eh Jack?"

Cameron nodded, thinking for a moment that his sibling was merely winding him up.

"But my dear Jack, you were only commissioned into the French army three months ago, and the dispatches bearing your details bound for Versailles haven't even been sent yet" said Callum smugly.

Cameron's heart sank, his brother knew about his woman, and when he had been promoted. How on earth could he know? He thought to ask but figured that his brother was going to tell him anyway.

Sure enough, Callum continued.

"In any case, you were in *the Pretender*'s life guard at Prestonpans and to the best of my knowledge, that is not a French unit, nor were you in the French service when you fought alongside the MacDonalds and Irish traitors at Falkirk and I'll wager those McPhersons you aided against his royal highness down at Clifton aren't French either".

Cameron was stunned and initially said nothing. How did the Hanoverians know this? He was surely going to hang as a traitor now, French commission or no French commission.

"Not going to be much use to your little Elgin whore when you're dancing on the end of a rope are you Jack?" added his brother, making Cameron's blood boil.

The regimental commander interrupted them.

"Well sir, I see you are not who you claim to have been, you are no French Officer but more a damn rebel dog, and a Papist one at that, guards take him away and find out all he knows"

"Let me interrogate the prisoner" pleaded Callum, the commander answered with a simple nod of the head.

Cameron was dragged out by the two sentries and taken towards the edge of the camp near some supply wagons. Here he was unceremoniously stripped of his beloved long red coat and tied to a wagon wheel by his ankles and wrists so tightly that he could barely move. The guards stole the coins and telescope from the pockets of his coat and ripped his shirt open but they spared him the indignity of rifling his trouser pockets. The next thing he saw was a fist crashing into his face, followed by a frenzied series of blows to his face and body. Winded and unable to move, Jack waited for the questions to come but the soldiers seemed content just to beat the living daylights out of him for the time being. The beating went on for what seemed like hours before Callum returned, still wearing the smug grin.

"Still need help to beat me up I see Callum, nothing ever changes eh?" said Cameron to his brother defiantly.

His brother answered him with another punch in the face before dismissing the two guards. Now it was just the two of them.

"Serving king George, mother and father would have been proud," said Cameron sarcastically, expecting another punch in the face, but it didn't come.

Callum just laughed aloud then said "I suppose you want to know how we know so much about you?"

"Not really" said Cameron, "There are spies everywhere".

Callum responded.

"Ah but this spy has been extremely helpful to us, how else would we know how short on cavalry and artillery your pathetic rebel army is? Or how you have a major ammunition shortage? Your army is even running out of food and money my dear brother".

Cameron was shocked that the enemy knew all this, he knew both sides had spies and that the government intelligence was a lot better than the Jacobites' but this lot seemed to know everything. Where were they getting such detailed information from? Cameron realised there must be a high level turncoat in the Jacobite army, but who? If only he could warn them.

"You're going to hang tomorrow, dear brother," said Callum "as all traitors eventually do" he added, with an evil smile.

"Even traitors to their rightful King and country who side with England?" growled Cameron.

Callum responded by punching his brother in the mouth, making him bleed, then saying "I could maybe swing it with the commander for you to join us and turn *King's evidence* against your rebel colleagues."

Cameron responded by summoning all his remaining strength to spit in Callums face, a deed that earned him another blow, this time to the stomach.

"Suit yourself dear brother" gloated Callum "maybe I'll pay Mary, that is her name isn't it? Yes maybe I'll pay Mary a visit when you're dead, I'm sure she'll be most accommodating" he sneered.

All Cameron could do was spit at him again and this time he was beaten unconscious by his younger brother. Everything went black.

CHAPTER TEN

HERE COMES THE CAVALRY

It was five am when Private O'Donnell and the remnants of the Irish company trudged back into Elgin utterly exhausted and demoralised. A low mist covered the surrounding hills and it was a lot colder than it should be in April, even in the highlands.

They were greeted by Sergeant McDermott and Private McHardy with the ten other men close behind. McDermott enquired as to the whereabouts of Captain Cameron and the ammunition and was soon told all about the massacre at the barn, the ambush at Braemuir, the slaughter of the clan Cameron detachment and of Jack Cameron's capture. The news of Cameron being taken captive lay heavy on the hearts of the Irish company, as did news of what had happened to the men of Elgin in the flaming barn.

Sergeant McDermott reluctantly conceded that they should now head back to the main Jacobite army at Inverness and the men started to put the wounded on makeshift stretchers. They were almost ready to move out of town when a sentry reported that a body of red-coated horsemen were riding along the track towards the town followed by a party of fifty highlanders. Sergeant McDermott ran in the direction the column was coming from, after ordering the men to conceal themselves in Elgin's houses and to wait for the order to fire. Reaching the town gates, McDermott was relieved to see that the red-coated horsemen were, in fact, the sole squadron of Fitz-James' horse, commanded by Cameron's friend, Lieutenant Caldwell. The clansmen behind them he recognised as being *Stewarts of Appin*. Sure that the approaching troops were friendly, McDermott waved a signal back to his men ordering them to stand down.

Saluting Lieutenant Caldwell as he came to a halt in front of him, McDermott proceeded to tell the Officer everything he had just been told about Cameron's mission and of his capture. He also told the redcoat Officer about the atrocity committed at the barn, news that enraged the Stewart men who had paused to rest and clean their muskets nearby. Lieutenant Caldwell seemed devastated that his friend had been captured.

Cameron and Caldwell had been in Fitz-James' together in Flanders and had great respect and admiration for each other. It had been Caldwell who had received the tip off about the ammunition store that had been in

Elgin. Caldwell seemed to be considering his options for a moment then promptly declared,

"Well boys, we need that ammunition and I don't know about you but I don't like the idea of a true Jacobite like Captain Cameron falling into their hands and being tortured, what say we go and rescue him?"

All the soldiers present answered in unison with a rousing "Aye".

Caldwell sent ten of the Stewarts back to Inverness with the Irish wounded and led the column, now over one hundred and fifty men strong, east, in the direction of Braemuir.

CHAPTER ELEVEN

NO WAY OUT

Cameron woke early that morning still tied tightly to the wagon wheel, his face a swollen and bloody mess, his mouth as dry as a bone and with hunger pangs in his stomach. He felt awful, and today he was going to hang. His guard offered him some water but when Cameron nodded, he simply had a bucket of icy water thrown over him. It still felt good on his wounds. He looked around and could see no sign of his twisted brother. He was left tied to the wheel without food or water but also without any further beatings, though he ominously saw a cavalryman hitching a nasty looking noose to the boughs of a tree at the other end of camp. All Cameron could do was think. He thought about his beloved Mary and what would become of her without him, her father or her brother to look after her. He thought about the poor clan Cameron men he had foolishly led into a slaughter at Braemuir, and about the company he had accidentally abandoned. In his head he could still hear the screams of the Cameron men as they were slaughtered by the rampant English cavalry and he vowed to himself that should he ever get out of his current situation he would never allow such a thing to happen again.

Not that he was going to get out of this. Jack Cameron had been in precarious situations before but this one took some beating. Then he remembered what his brother had said about the spy in the Jacobite army. They simply had to be warned. Who the hell was sharing their secrets with the Hanoverians? If only he could escape and warn them. Thinking of this breathed new life into his broken spirit and Cameron was overjoyed to notice that the bonds that held one of his hands had slackened a little. Not much, but a little. It must have been the seemingly endless beatings from the guards and his brother that had loosened them. Not loose enough to escape though, even though there was only one sentry nearby. His beautiful Mary flashed into his head once more and he recalled their final parting when they had gazed lovingly into each other's eyes and she had given him her brooch. The brooch! He had forgotten about that! His dim guards had neglected to search his trousers after they had relieved him of his coat. Cameron wriggled and rubbed away with his wrists but couldn't quite get to it. If only he could loosen his bonds. Then he had an idea.

CHAPTER TWELVE

A SCORE TO SETTLE

The Irish company and Fitz-James' made good progress towards Braemuir with their Stewart allies. Moving in broad daylight with Fitz-James' acting as an advance guard, they soon reached the barn and the hastily dug graves beside it, each man removing his headgear as he passed, in respect for the murdered civilians. Lieutenant Caldwell was relishing the chase and seemed very eager to catch up with their quarry and free his friend. The enlisted men felt the same. They travelled quickly through the rolling heather and over the steep braes for a time until they reached Braemuir, the sight of Cameron's rash, ill-fated assault on the Campbell militia unit.

The Cameron bodies had been stripped and left for the crows by the Campbells so the Irish company with the Stewart men stopped to bury them too. Private O'Donnell said a few words of prayer and everyone present made the sign of the cross but O'Donnell noticed that Lieutenant Caldwell looked shaken and uneasy during the brief memorial service.

O'Donnell pointed in the direction the enemy had taken Cameron and they headed off with all speed over the far ridge and into a small wooded glen. The troopers of Fitz-James' had to go in single file due to the narrow track so the column snaked through the glen like a tartan and red serpent looking for its prey. After about an hour, the men could see an open field at the end of the glen, surrounded by a stone wall and they advanced to within one thousand yards of it before Caldwell sent O'Donnell and McHardy forward to see if the enemy were around. They were greeted with a startling, yet, promising sight.

In the field were two wagons loaded with barrels, each wagon having a split wheel that had obviously been damaged when it had been dragged through the glen. Beside the wagons sat a group of clansmen cleaning muskets and sharpening swords while they ate what looked like a roasted bullock cooked on a spit. The meat smelt terrific to McHardy and O'Donnell. O'Donnell recognised the men as being the Campbells they had encountered before, though he could not see William Campbell, the vile ginger-haired, scarred leader of the unit.

The two men crept back to the rest of their small column with this news, pointing out to Caldwell that the Argyle men had foolishly taken no precautions and placed no sentries. For a man who was determined to rescue his friend, Caldwell seemed a tad concerned that they had found these particular men and he seemed to drift into his own thoughts for a moment when he was told that their leader was not present. After considering this and considering the fact that they probably wouldn't be able to take the ammunition back to Inverness even if they recaptured it, Caldwell suddenly decided that they would attack the Campbells immediately. He ordered the Irish company and the Stewart men, all of whom were thirsting for revenge, to creep forward and give the Campbells a volley or three while he himself would circle around with his small cavalry force and attack them from the flank, hopefully catching them in a pincer movement. Orders were relayed and the men eagerly took up their positions. Sergeant McDermott suggested that they take some prisoners so as to gain information on Captain Cameron's whereabouts but this suggestion curiously seemed to incense Caldwell who replied that the men were murderers and should all be killed.

The plan was that the Irish company and the Stewarts would stay hidden until the Campbells saw Fitz-James' charge, before delivering their volleys, as it was hoped the Campbells would present easy targets when they rose to flee from the formidable Irish horsemen.

The men edged into position and waited.

Ten minutes later the troopers of Fitz-James' came galloping out of the trees to the left of the field towards the Campbells, whooping and yelling, waving their terrifying heavy cavalry sabres. It had the desired effect. The leaderless Campbells rose up in disorder and tried to flee but a thunderous volley from the Stewarts and the Irish company mowed half of them down. Two of the Campbells managed to mount horses that had been obscured by the wagons and rode off but they were pursued by Caldwell and two troopers, while the remaining Campbells had to face the bayonet charge of the Irish and the highland charge of the Stewarts and their broadswords. With a cry of "Claymore" the Stewart men dropped their muskets and rushed in with their basket hilted broadswords, while the Irish company fixed bayonets and charged too, Sergeant McDermott screaming *"Erin go Bragh"* as he plunged his bayonet into his first adversary.

The Campbell men were tough when fighting alongside Hanoverian regulars or bullying defenceless civilians but against this ferocious onslaught they stood no chance. It was all over in minutes. Only two Campbells had loaded muskets and they accounted for the only Jacobite casualties of the skirmish, gunning down two Stewarts who had charged too early but they, and the rest of their Argyle kin, soon all lay dead. Three Campbells who tried to run at the end of the fight were mercilessly cut down by the men of Fitz-James' and within ten minutes of the troopers' initial charge all the Campbells lay dead, save for the two who had been chased off by Caldwell and two of his men. The Stewart men buried their dead and carried on with the tradition of robbing the Campbell corpses, whom everyone refused to bury.

Private O'Donnell had a wound on his shoulder but was in high spirits after the victory, declaring to McDermott that he wished they had taken the Campbells' leader too. McDermott replied, "We'll get him next time, maybe Caldwell or Captain Cameron already have." The men piled their enemies' arms and took the standard precaution of posting sentries, something that their late opponents would have done well to remember to do.

Private McHardy examined the ammunition cart for a few moments then burst into fits of laughter that were soon tempered by a melancholy realisation that their original mission had been a fools errand. "What's so funny McHardy?" asked McDermott.

McHardy was the best shot in the regiment. Not quite the dirty street fighter that O'Donnell was, nor the lead from the front hero type like McDermott, but he was indeed a crack shot and a fiercely patriotic Scot and ardent Jacobite. He had been in the Irish brigade longer than anyone else in the detachment other than O'Donnell and his knowledge and experience were well respected. McDermott reiterated his question to McHardy who examined the contents of the wagons again before answering.

"This is bloody British ammunition sir" he exclaimed, "It's no good to us. No wonder these pro government dogs stole it, they needed it for themselves."

McDermott, in turn, examined the ammo and concluded that McHardy was, as usual, absolutely right. British musket balls were of a larger *calibre* than those used by their French enemies and since every soldier in the Jacobite army carried a French musket, or *carbine* in case of the cavalry, it was utterly useless to them. Their original mission had been a waste of time. British troops could, in desperation, use French balls but they were too small and would either be wildly inaccurate in the larger British muzzle or could misfire making the musket explode. British ammunition on the other hand simply wouldn't fit down the *muzzle* of a French musket.

There was still no sign of Caldwell and his two troopers after an hour so McDermott decided that they would wait an hour longer then proceed without him. Where was Lieutenant Caldwell?

CHAPTER THIRTEEN

A GIFT FROM THE GODS

Cameron struggled in vain with his bonds once more then decided he must give his plan a try. He was going to hang anyway so he had nothing to lose. He remembered how the awful beating he had received had slowly loosed his bonds with every impact but they were still just too tight. He needed another beating. He waited until the brutal sentry who had doled out the majority of his punishment the previous evening walked past, and he spat on the soldier's freshly washed tunic. The sentry stopped and stared at Cameron in utter disbelief before thumping the stock of his musket into Cameron's groin. It was agony but Cameron summoned up a deep breath and shouted "God and King James" at the now irate soldier who hit Cameron with a frenzy of blows to his head and body before Cameron slumped down, apparently unconscious.

Cameron waited until he was sure the guard had gone before once more trying to loosen his bonds. It had worked! His left hand was loose! Checking to see that no guards were looking, he reached down and grabbed the beautiful brooch that Mary had given him from his pocket. He quickly used the sharp pin to cut his other hand free then reached down and loosened his tied ankles, being careful to keep them looking as if they were still tied tight. He needed a weapon and boots if he was going to have any chance of escape. He saw the brutal sentry march past again, doing his rounds, and decided to go for it. It was now or never.

"God bless King James, Prince Charles and the Pope" boomed Cameron.

It had the desired effect. The guard tramped over and raised the butt of his gun ready to strike Cameron again but this time Cameron brushed aside his bonds and rammed the brooch pin into the guard's throat. Cameron was lucky. The guard's mouth filled with blood, leaving him unable to make any sound with his mouth to raise the alarm.

As the stunned guard gurgled and tried to turn his musket to shoot Cameron, Cameron quickly drew the guard's own sabre and with all his might rammed it into the guard's side, puncturing his lungs and making him unable to scream. The guard collapsed in a heap without being able to fire his musket, which Cameron duly grabbed.

Deciding that he had no time to steal the man's boots, Cameron made a rush for the trees in his bare feet, not stopping until he has nearly half a mile away. While running he heard a shot being fired in the camp as someone discovered the dead guard but even with his feet being cut to ribbons on stones and nettles, Cameron knew he had got away. He had been lucky. Very lucky. He slung the loaded musket over his shoulder and continued running west, back towards Braemuir.

Cameron ran and ran. He felt like his heart was going to explode but all he could think about now was getting back to Inverness to warn the Jacobite army about the traitor in their midst and to eventually get back to his beloved Mary. Oh how that brooch had come in useful!

Cameron stuck to wooded areas as best he could so as to avoid detection and he made good progress despite his fatigue, his wounds and his bare feet. When he judged that there was no one on his tail, he decided it was necessary to stop and drink when he found a small stream running through the trees. The water tasted like nectar itself to the tall Officer and he drank his fill before hurriedly pressing on westwards through the woods. Ahead, Cameron could see a small clearing so he slowed his pace a little so as to avoid detection from any would be enemies. He edged forward slowly until he reached the clearing's edge where he saw a strange worrying site. On the floor of the clearing were two dead redcoats. When he was sure no one else was around, he crept closer and to his astonishment he found them to be wearing the red coats of Fitz-James'. The two men's horses were nowhere to be seen so he decided to look a little closer. Close examination revealed that one man had been shot in the back at seemingly point blank range while the other had been beheaded, his head lying a few feet away.

This puzzled Cameron. Were they taken by surprise?

Why were they so far east?

Where were the rest of their squadron?

Cameron relieved one of the men of his boots and carried on westwards, still puzzled as to the fate of these two troopers but still desperately wanting to get back to his men and warn the army about the spy. His good friend, Lieutenant Caldwell, commanded the men he had just found, Cameron thanked god and Jesus that it wasn't his body he had found. Maybe Caldwell knew who the spy was. Cameron trudged on.

Being from Edinburgh, Cameron greatly appreciated the beautiful scenery of the highlands, the purple heather and the smell of the forest. He was tired now and his pace slowed a little until he came to a small wooden bridge that spanned a babbling burn. Not wanting to take any chances, he decided to rest under the bridge to avoid detection. It felt good to rest and for the first time since being captured he felt like he was finally going to make it. His elation was short lived as he heard horses approaching from two different directions. Cameron decided to stay put as he only had one shot and no bayonet with which to defend himself. He squinted through a small gap in the bridge's woodwork and the sight he saw filled him with horror and a venomous rage at the same time. Three men were standing next to the bridge talking.

CHAPTER FOURTEEN

DUPLICITY

Cameron's blood boiled as he listened to the three figures talking together. Standing beside the bridge were the vile William Campbell, his own brother, Callum Cameron and Lieutenant Caldwell of Fitz-James'! At first Cameron didn't want to believe that his old friend Caldwell was a traitor and spy. It made no sense. Caldwell was an ardent Jacobite and a true Scot who, like Cameron, despised the union and longed for the day that Scotland could be free again. They had charged *British squares* together in Flanders when Cameron was also a trooper in Fitz-James', they had raided Austrian supply columns in the name off King Louis and they had both sworn an oath of allegiance both to France and to the exiled Stuarts.

Maybe Caldwell had been sent to parley with the enemy, thought Cameron, or maybe they were arranging a short truce or perhaps a prisoner exchange. Cameron had no choice for the moment but to stay still and quiet and to listen. The first voice he heard was that of his Hanoverian brother.

"So, Caldwell what have you got for us today? And it had better be good."

Cameron was utterly shocked to hear Caldwell reply.

"Well sir the rebels are in sorry shape indeed. They are desperately short of ammunition and food and it looks like our navy did us a great service depriving them of that gold." Caldwell was referring to the earlier loss of le prince Charles, the French ship lost carrying the latest shipment of money bound for the Jacobite army.

He continued.

"They are also woefully short of horse, two squadrons at the most, their other cavalry units now serve as foot."

"Yes yes we already know all this Caldwell" interrupted Callum Cameron, "anything else?"

Caldwell replied.

"Yes sir, around fifteen hundred of the Pretender's best highlanders are deployed far to the west of Inverness with some of their artillery. I'll wager if his royal highness attacks now he could catch the rebels off balance and under strength."

"You're not paid to think Caldwell, you're paid to spy" ranted Callum but at the same time he seemed interested that the rebels at Inverness were so under strength.

"There's something else sir" added Caldwell.

"The rebels have been forced to pay their men in meal rather than gold for the aforementioned reasons and their last substantial meal store is in Inverness."

Callum needed no further information, he knew that if Cumberland and the Hanoverian army advanced toward Inverness, the rebels would have no option but to stand and fight, whatever their condition, for fear of their army melting away through want and lack of pay. Cameron could not believe what he was hearing, his friend of many years and comrade in arms, a traitor! But there was more.

"I assume you have been re-acquainted with your brother sir" quipped Caldwell "did you remember our agreement?" he added "he was not to be harmed."

"You don't make demands Caldwell. I'm going to see that treacherous brother of mine hang, today, as it goes. I did offer him the chance to side with us but the stubborn Papist fool refused" said Callum, dryly, before asking Caldwell.

"So how did you get away to make contact?"

Caldwell answered by saying that it hadn't been easy as some highlanders had been attached to his squadron and he had unexpectedly bumped into Jack's company in Elgin which Callum and Campbell had assured him would be destroyed. Cameron listened as the plot unfolded. Caldwell was supposed to have led his squadron into a trap that only he would be the survivor off, thus depriving the Jacobites of half their cavalry force and essentially blinding their army, as Fitz-James' were, by now, providing all the rebel army's reconnaissance. He hadn't, however, figured on bumping into the Irish company and having to take a different route east to rescue Cameron and retrieve the ammunition lost from Elgin. When Caldwell told Callum and Campbell about wiping out Campbell's militia company earlier, Cameron heard Campbell draw a sword and scream insults but he also heard his brother intervene.

"Now William, you know your men were expendable, you will soon be rewarded for your loyalty" patronised Callum. Caldwell continued by telling how he had slipped away to make contact by accompanying two of his troopers in pursuit of the two mounted Campbell fugitives, and waited until his men had cut them down before turning back with them to supposedly rejoin the Irish company. They had stopped briefly in a clearing and dismounted on Caldwell's orders to answer a call of nature and he had shot one and beheaded the other, stampeding their horses. It turned out that Caldwell had known the ammunition the Irish company had been sent for was British and largely useless to the Jacobites, it had all been a ruse by Cameron's brother to ensnare him. The ammunition was really going to be used to arm pro government militia.

Cameron seethed with rage. His friend was no more than a cowardly murdering, money grabbing, traitorous spy, little better than his brother. He wanted to show himself and kill all three of them but knew it would be suicide. He heard the jingle of money as Callum threw bags of coins to Campbell and Caldwell before mounting his horse and riding off. When his brother was gone, Cameron heard Campbell and Caldwell start to argue about the slaughter of the Argyle men, and the argument soon degenerated into threats. Cameron heard them start to fight with swords.

Squinting through a gap in the bridge's framework, Cameron could see that Campbell was having the better of the fight, thanks to his *targe*, a round leather and wood shield. Though he now hated Caldwell, he still wanted him to win, not only because he wished to see Caldwell brought to justice at Inverness, but also because of what the vile Campbell had done to his lover, Mary.

Cameron saw his chance as the fight moved the men a little farther away and he got up and made a run for it, westward. The two men stopped fighting when they saw Cameron and instantly levelled their firearms, Campbell his brace of pistols, Caldwell reaching into his saddle for his carbine. Cameron felt three shots whiz past him, one snapping a branch, inches from his face. Only Caldwell was mounted and as Cameron only had one shot, he decided it was prudent to down Caldwell's horse to make good his escape. Cameron turned and aimed at the horses belly before squeezing the trigger and sending the beast to equine heaven. Caldwell was thrown from his horse, dazed and ruffled but otherwise unhurt but Campbell kept up a hot pursuit. Campbell chased Cameron for a good four hundred yards before the exhausted Cameron felt he had no option but to turn and fight but with no cartridges, all he could do was use his empty musket like a club. Cameron decided to put a tree between himself and the evil ginger clansman. He skilfully dodged three broadsword thrusts from Campbell and parried a fourth with his empty gun before lady luck threw him a lifeline. A fifth thrust by Campbell imbedded itself in the tree Cameron was using to dodge the blows and Cameron seized his chance by whacking the sword with his musket, snapping the blade off at the hilt and rendering it useless. A second later, he booted Campbell in the groin and then again in the face when he doubled over with pain. Grabbing the broken clansman from behind he reached back into his pocket for the brooch given to him by Mary that he had used to kill the guard back at the camp of Kingston's horse. It was stained with the guard's blood and he slashed it right across Campbell's throat, growling in his ear "That's for Mary and the men of Elgin you Bastard" before spitting in his face and letting him drop to the ground dead. He took Campbell's *dirk* and two pistols which he quickly loaded from the dead man's cartridge pouch. He was not a second too soon, for as he spun around he saw his friend, Lieutenant Caldwell, aiming his now reloaded carbine at him. "I'm sorry Jack but it has to be this way," said Caldwell.

Cameron just stared at his old friend and asked, "Why did you do it?"

Caldwell answered.

"I did it for the money Jack. And because I couldn't stand exile in France anymore." Caldwell re-aimed his carbine and again said, "I'm sorry Jack."

Cameron thought he was going to die.

CHAPTER FIFTEEN

REDEMPTION

The sound of hooves coming along the track made Caldwell lower his weapon as twelve men of Fitz-James' rode up as if from nowhere alongside them. Caldwell couldn't kill Cameron now but he was flabbergasted when Cameron piped up to the troopers.

"Lieutenant Caldwell rescued me," boomed Cameron, which the troopers answered with a short 'hurrah'. As Cameron was senior officer, Caldwell could do nothing in front of the men except pretend to be flummoxed by their admiration and when Cameron mounted Caldwell's horse there was nothing for Caldwell to do except hitch a lift with one of his troopers, back to the wagons, back to the Irish company.

Caldwell was puzzled by Cameron's behaviour. Why had he said nothing to the troopers? The mounted party rode hell for leather back to the small glen where the wagons and the rest of the Irish company waited with the Stewarts. The men, who had been about to leave if the last mounted patrol had returned empty-handed, greeted them warmly. Cameron was glad to see his men again, though he looked odd in just his shirt without his own musket and sword.

"We must return to the army at Inverness now" boomed Cameron "There is a traitor in the army and we must warn the Prince".

Cameron saw Caldwell go as white as a sheet but he again said nothing more as the men made ready to leave. Caldwell wondered what Cameron had in store for him. Cameron and McDermott decided that, since the ammunition could neither be moved, thanks to its broken wagon wheels, nor used thanks to its excessive calibre, that it should be destroyed, blown up.

Privates McHardy and O'Donnell set to work laying fuses but they were interrupted when two Fitz –James' troopers, who had been posted to a far ridge, came galloping in with worrying news. A huge body of Argyle militia were advancing from the east and would soon be upon them. Cameron had to think fast.

He knew Caldwell would fancy his chances of escaping during a fight but he couldn't expose him as a traitor to the men for fear of sapping their morale at this crucial stage of the mission. The troopers reported at least three hundred militiamen were heading their way and would be upon them shortly. Sure that Hanoverian regulars would be close behind,

Cameron decided that staying to fight would be suicide, but they had to destroy the ammunition before it could fall into enemy hands, then he had an idea.

Cameron asked Caldwell to walk with him a moment until they were out of earshot of the men.

"Will you turn me in Jack?" asked Caldwell.

"It doesn't make any sense to me at all David" replied Cameron.

"Ok so you hated exile and needed the money but I've known you for many years. There must be more to this treachery."

Caldwell bowed his head and briefly filled Cameron in. Caldwell had family in Glasgow who were well to do traders. A government spy had found out that the family had a relative in the French service and that his regiment had been sent to Scotland to aid the Jacobites. Through his family they had ensured that he knew if he didn't turn spy against his own army, his family would be dispossessed and transported to the West Indies as slaves. Cameron sympathised a little but went further

"That doesn't explain how you were receiving English gold David, why would they pay someone they were blackmailing?"

Caldwell answered bluntly that a merchant from Elgin had somehow found out about his secret and had been blackmailing him, threatening to blow his cover if he didn't pay up. The English had agreed to pay the blackmailer for him to safeguard their intelligence but had later decided to kill of Elgin's market traders so as to not take any chances. That's why they had been burned by the Campbells in the barn.

Caldwell had refused to inform his blackmailers who the merchant was, as the merchant's name was Donald Kerr, Mary's father, and he did no want Cameron's woman to lose her father as he knew how Jack felt about her. Caldwell added that he was sure Mary had known nothing of this. Cameron instinctively knew his old friend was telling the truth. He was sure.

But this revelation had put Cameron in an awful predicament.

"So David what am I to do? He asked.

"Do I tell your men you were going to have them all killed and that you murdered two of their comrades? Do I tell my men they've been fighting and dying in the middle of bloody nowhere for no good reason? Do I take you back to Inverness and let the army hang you as a traitor? I know you can't run back to the English as they'll think you killed William

Campbell and in any case you're no good to them with your cover blown, what am I to do with you?"

Caldwell asked Cameron for a pistol so he could at least die like a gentleman but Cameron had another idea. "There's a huge band of vengeful Campbells closing in David, we must run, not fight, and we must destroy this ammunition and get safely back to warn the army. I need those Campbells slowed down. Do you know of any man who would be willing to do this? Any loyal Jacobite Scottish man?"

Caldwell made a resigned smile at his old friend and declared "Oh yes Jack, I know of one such man"

The Irish company and the Stewarts formed a column and began to march west as fast as they could. Fitz-James' horse were sent galloping away ahead with orders simply to rejoin the army as quickly as possible. They were without their officer. Cameron waited behind and saw the Campbell militia crest the small rise at the far end of the glen. Cameron and Caldwell shook hands and Caldwell added "I see you lost your sword, please take mine, I won't need it" and he handed Cameron the basket hilted broadsword and its scabbard that he had been using for the last while.

"Thank you David, god be with you" said Cameron.

"God and King James" replied Caldwell with a smile. Cameron sprinted off to rejoin his comrades on the road back to Inverness.

CHAPTER SIXTEEN

HONOUR

Caldwell, now without a sword, stood alone beside the two ammunition wagons that had caused so much trouble. He had Cameron's two pistols loaded and another four loaded muskets beside him, as well as another six loaded pistols inside the wagon that contained most of the powder and shot. He waited until the Campbells were within one hundred yards before opening fire with the muskets. Only forty or so Campbells had advanced towards him as they had seen that only one man was left behind. His first four shots downed three men then he emptied the two pistols given him by Cameron into the advancing Argyle men before jumping into the wagon. For a time the Argyle men stood aghast at this seemingly crazed man who wore the uniform of France but who roared insults and challenges at them in a coarse Scots accent. He took a musket ball in the stomach and one in his arm before he could down another two men with the extra loaded pistols. He was soon overrun, Campbell men starting to poke the injured man's wounds with broadswords as they surrounded the wagons and mocked him. His last act was to hold an empty pistol up to the short, short fuse that O'Donnell and McHardy had made next to the powder and pull the trigger. The spark ignited the powder causing an almighty explosion that killed Caldwell and a good twenty of his opponents instantly, wounding many more with flying wooden splinters and shot.

Cameron and his men, now a good distance away, turned when they heard the huge explosion and cheered the brave Lieutenant Caldwell. Cameron felt grief at the loss of his friend but was proud that he had regained some of his tarnished honour with this defiant last stand.

"God and King James" murmured Cameron to himself. The column marched on back to Inverness.

The journey through the glens and up and down the braes back to the Jacobite base at Inverness seemed to take an eternity for Cameron. What had started as a relatively simple mission to scavenge some ammunition and visit his lover had turned into quite a compact mini campaign. The loss of Caldwell lay heavy on his heart, as did his friend's revelations about Mary's father and the blackmail. Mary would no doubt be distraught at the news, though Cameron suspected that the people of

Elgin already knew what was going to happen when the enemy had arrived in town and rounded up all of the men.

Caldwell, on the other hand, was a different kettle of fish altogether. Cameron simply hadn't seen that treachery coming, especially from a man of previously good character whom he had fought alongside in Flanders and known for many years. Should he inform his superior, Brigadier Stapleton, about Caldwell's duplicity or should he keep quiet, knowing that the spy was now neutralised? News that an Officer of one of the Franco-Irish units was a traitor would no doubt cause great loss of morale in the army as well as mutual mistrust between them and the Scottish units. This would be catastrophic at this stage of the war. The rank and file seemed to get on well enough with each other but Cameron knew that things weren't so rosy between the army's *Franco-Irish Officers* and the clan chiefs. Mutual mistrust, since the retreat from Derby had bubbled away between the army's commanders and the Prince and this had contributed to the farcical way in which the army had been organised since it retreated into the highlands after the battle of Falkirk. Should he tell Stapleton?

CHAPTER SEVENTEEN

HOME FOR THE NIGHT?

The tiny column marched back into the main Jacobite camp at Inverness that night. They received a hero's welcome from the blue-coated troopers of the Prince's lifeguard who had escorted them from the town of Inverness to the new camp site around the grounds of nearby Culloden house, a few miles outside the town. They were initially challenged in the dark by the horsemen but were soon exchanging news with them about the army's current state of affairs. One piece of news was greeted enthusiastically by the men. Cumberland's government army had left Aberdeen and crossed the Spey without any opposition. It was widely expected that they would arrive to do battle tomorrow, April 15th. Sergeant McDermott started to wind the men up as they began to pitch their tents for the night.

"We're going to really give it to these bastards tomorrow lads, *Erin go Bragh*" he boomed." Remember Falkirk and Fontenoy!"

Cameron saw the men were delighted to be reunited with the rest of their red coated comrades and they made a much more formidable body of men when numbering one hundred and fifty muskets. Along with the three hundred men of the army's only other regular infantry contingent, the blue coated Royal Ecossaise, they were going to have to provide much of the firepower tomorrow while the clan regiments sought their traditional mass charge against the government ranks. Cameron was invited to a council of war the next day at dawn with Brigadier Stapleton and the army's other senior Officers. The warm welcome he and his men had received upon returning from their mission had made his mind up not to say anything about Caldwell other than that he had died bravely sacrificing himself so his comrades in arms could escape. Looking around camp, even in the dark, it looked as if there were barely half the number of troops who had fought at Falkirk three months earlier and rumour had it that the Hanoverian army on it's way to do battle with them the next day was ten thousand men strong. He wasn't going to do anything to affect their morale. The men threw themselves down to grab some well-earned sleep. Tomorrow would bring battle.

The next morning gave Captain Cameron and his men the chance to assess the dispositions of the rest of their army and an opportunity to see the battlefield where they would take on the Hanoverian forces that day. Cameron and McDermott weren't impressed. The Prince and his advisors had chosen what looked like a plain flat moor for the coming battle. Plain flat moors were ideal for set piece continental style battles between regular forces of foot, horse and artillery, but only one army that was due to participate in this showdown was comprised like that and it certainly wasn't this one. McDermott voiced his concerns about the choice of battlefield declaring "I see this is where the fate of our enterprise will be decided."

Cameron agreed with his red haired Sergeant. The plain flat moor offered every possible advantage to the conventional Hanoverian forces. Plenty of room to use their cavalry on the flanks, reasonably flat ground on which to deploy their ranks of infantry and a clear unobstructed field of fire for their cannon. In contrast, the field offered little to the Jacobite army. Their best shock troops, the highland units, would have to charge across open ground under fire and if this rain kept up they would be advancing through a quagmire. The Jacobites only had two squadrons of cavalry available in the shape of Fitz-James' and the Prince's life guards, a paltry one hundred and fifty horsemen in comparison to the Hanoverians, whom spies had told the Jacobite high command had around thirteen hundred cavalry. Cameron and McDermott were forced to end their discussion when Stapleton's *ADC* arrived to inform Cameron that his presence was requested at the council of war. He and McDermott would have to review their dispositions later.

The Jacobites had commandeered Culloden house, usually a residence of the pro government Duncan Forbes of Culloden but, for the time being, it was serving as the Jacobites' main command post.

Cameron was taken to the room where the council of war was being held, passing beautiful paintings and magnificent chandeliers that gave the mansion an almost regal feel. In the council room, standing around a table, were the Jacobite commanders and some of the army's senior and most experienced Officers. The men were stood around a crude map of the area stretched out on the table. Cameron took his place next to his superior, Brigadier Stapleton. The leaders were arguing. Cameron recognised his Prince who stood strangely quiet while the others ranted and argued. He also noted that Lords Strathallan and *Elcho* were present, who commanded Strathallan's horse and the Prince's lifeguard respectively. Also present were *Lord George Murray*, Sheridan and *O'Sullivan*, the Prince's two Irish military advisors, Donald Cameron, chief of the Camerons of Lochiel and a few of the other clan chiefs. There was a heated debate going on.

Lord George Murray was bitterly opposed to fighting on Drummossie Moor, the chosen battlefield, as he knew the field's unsuitability for highland troops. Murray was for retreating to more favourable ground that would suit the highland charge better and that would neutralise the Hanoverians undoubted numerical superiority. The chiefs, for the most part, seemed to be agreeing with Murray. Murray's argument was falling on deaf ears though. The Irish Officers, O'Sullivan and Sheridan, seemed determined that they should fight here at Culloden, citing fairly obvious reasons. They had, after all, already defeated two Hanoverian armies sent against them and they, and crucially the Prince, saw no reason why their superb highland infantry could not triumph a third time. In any case, argued O'Sullivan, with gold running out and the men being paid in meal, the army simply had to make a stand so that they could retain their last remaining meal store in Inverness, just down the road. Without any means to pay the army it would likely melt away. Murray agreed that they had indeed enjoyed considerable success previously against the Hanoverians but that this had been influenced by circumstance just as much as by the bravery of the clans.

Cameron admired Murray. Tough and uncompromising, he seemed to know instinctively the best way to use highland troops, though at times he could be stubborn and ignore advice. Murray certainly had a point too, not just about the inappropriate choice of battlefield but about how circumstance had favoured them in the two previous victories. At Prestonpans they had triumphed thanks to an outflanking manoeuvre and by virtue of the facts that the Hanoverian horse had ran away and the infantry and artillery were poorly led, poorly organised and inexperienced. At Falkirk, the victory had been much harder won and had been made easier by the fact that the enemy had deployed no artillery and that its cavalry had again fled through their own lines causing panic and disruption. Crucially also, in both previous engagements, the Jacobites and Hanoverians had roughly the same amount of men. This would not be the case at Culloden as a good fifteen hundred of the best Jacobite highlanders including the elite six hundred men of McPherson of Cluny's regiment who had fought so fiercely at Clifton were away on other missions tackling pro government clans and besieging those highland forts still in government hands to the west. They would not be back in time, argued Murray. Lochiel pointed out that no one had bothered sending carts to Inverness for supplies so the men were short of both ammunition and food, the days ration being a mere one biscuit per man. He added that many of his men had disappeared in an attempt to find food.

"A starving ill-supplied army is in no shape to fight," argued Murray. O'Sullivan replied, saying that if the men were in no fit state to fight they were in no fit state to withdraw either. The debate raged while Cameron bit his tongue. He was after all, only a Captain, and it was not his place to comment on general strategy. Then Cameron's commander, Brigadier Stapleton, piped up "I think our highland friends prefer flight to fight". Cameron knew that would do it. However hopeless their chances were, they were now going to fight here as the clan chiefs would not tolerate this insult to their courage and loyalty. Sure enough, one by one, the chiefs indicated their willingness to stay and fight at Culloden, whatever the disparity between their own forces and the enemy, their one shred of hope being knowledge that they had already beaten the Hanoverian regulars twice.

Lord George Murray reluctantly agreed adding "never mind, we'll soon be putting an end to a bad affair" before storming out. Captain Cameron and the other officers were ordered to prepare their men for battle on *Drummossie moor* to await the arrival of the enemy.

Walking through the camp to rejoin his men, Cameron took stock of the situation around him. He could judge there to be no more than six thousand men under arms here, the vast majority of which were infantry. The army was ordered to draw up in two main battle lines with a small mounted reserve. They were to be drawn up between two sets of farms and walled enclosures on either flank. Cameron and his fellow Officers wanted the walls ripped down or, to at least have them garrisoned, as they could provide protection from any Hanoverian forces wishing to subject the Jacobites to flanking or enfilade fire. No orders came from the high command either to demolish the walls or to garrison the enclosures however, largely thanks to O'Sullivan's hare brained reasoning that the walls were "between us and them".

Between those walls in the front line holding the right flank was the experienced Atholl brigade, commanded by Lord George Murray consisting of four hundred men of Jack's namesake regiment clan Cameron, five hundred men of the Atholl brigade and two hundred and fifty men of the Stewart's of Appin, some of whom had helped Cameron and his men ambush the Campbells and the erroneous ammunition wagons. Murray had curiously been relieved of command of the whole army, his place taken by the Prince himself. The Prince had never commanded an army before.

The centre, under Lord Drummond, consisted of four hundred Frasers, three hundred and fifty men of clan Chattan, two hundred and fifty Farquarsons, two hundred and ninety Macleans, one hundred and fifty each of Chisholms and Macleods and two hundred men of John Roy Stewarts' Edinburgh regiment.

The left was made up entirely of Macdonald men of Clanranald's, Keppoch's and Glengarry's numbering around nine hundred men.

Though all of the men in the front line carried French firearms, some of the better off men were also armed with basket hilted broadswords and a round shield or targe, swords not unlike the magnificent weapon given to Cameron by his late friend Caldwell.

Cameron's Irish brigade held the extreme left of the second line. There had been three hundred of them initially but the siege of Stirling castle, the battle of Falkirk, disease, desertion and skirmishes like the ones fought by Cameron and his men in the past few days had thinned their ranks to a mere one hundred and fifty. Their commander, Major Summan, was ill with a fever so command of the Irish brigade nominally fell to Brigadier Stapleton, but his duties also included overall command of the second line so it was left to Cameron to lead the men initially.

To their right stood the Royal Ecossaise under Louis Drummond, brother of the Drummond who commanded the front centre. There had been five hundred of them but like the Irish Brigade they too had been worn down by time and duty to a mere three hundred. They wore blue coats with white cross belts and were armed like their Irish comrades with French muskets and bayonets, and these were the only two units who had full cartridge boxes holding twenty four rounds per man. The ranks of the Royal Ecossaise's second battalion had been swelled by a few Dozen deserters from Cumberland's army who could expect brutal justice if taken prisoner by their former employers.

To their right stood the two clan Gordon regiments and the Duke of Perth's regiment which held the extreme right of the second line.

A sort of third line stood behind them. The Prince's blue coated mounted life guards and Fitz-James' horse were both at squadron strength, around seventy men apiece and they were joined by Baggot's hussars, Lord Pitsligo's horse and Kilmarnock's horse, but there were no horses to accommodate these three units so they stood on foot. Eight artillery pieces of varying calibre were placed between the front line units, manned not by gunners but by a mix of highlanders and lowlanders who knew little or nothing of how to use them effectively.

The terrain to the front left oblique of the line looked boggy and more uneven than the rest and the line was not completely straight. To the front and right around two hundred yards in front of the right wing stood the other walled enclosure, also unmanned and still intact while the right rear of the army was partially protected by a deep sunken road.

Captain Cameron watched the rest of the army move into position. He protested to Stapleton that his rash outburst in the council of war had forced them to fight on this ground and that the experienced Irish brigade and the Royal Ecossaise should be in the front to utilise their superior firepower since it seemed to be a defensive action the army's commanders sought. Stapleton dismissed his protests but rather than reprimand him for insubordination he told him to take full command of the Irish brigade in the coming action. Cameron felt a warm glow of pride inside as he returned to his unit and started to check the men's weapons, making sure their muskets all had flints, dog head screws, clean muzzles and that every man had his twenty four rounds of ammunition.

Sergeant McDermott, as the brigade's senior sergeant, took pride knowing his Captain would lead the whole unit in the coming fight and he eagerly relayed this news to the men who cheered enthusiastically for their tall brave Captain who was now sporting a new red coat. They could put four hundred and fifty shots a minute into the air between them and though the odds were against their small army, they had every confidence in their own abilities and their own leader.

The army was now in position. It was starting to rain and an icy wind swirled around the moor, making the heather sway and making the place seem that little bit more isolated and desolate. Here they would fight. Here they would win or lose. Here they would live or die. They waited for the large government army to appear in the distance, coming from their camp at Nairn a mere twelve miles away. Any minute now they would see the columns of red coats and hear the beating of battalion drums in front of them, edging closer. They waited. And waited. And waited...

CHAPTER EIGHTEEN

A STAB IN THE DARK

Hours passed. It soon became glaringly obvious to all present that the Hanoverian army would not be coming to do battle today. All the army could see was the empty moor in front of them and no sign of the red-coated government troops they longed to fight. After another brief Officers' call the men were stood down. What biscuits were left were handed out to the men though a great many got nothing to eat and were forced to wander off to find what sustenance they could in the surrounding countryside. Cameron addressed his men.

"Well boys it looks like the enemy won't be gracing us with their presence today, stand down and take it easy, McHardy and Brown go and sort out some firewood for tonight." "Yes Captain" grumbled the two soldiers as they trudged off towards the rear carrying crude axes, their muskets slung over their shoulders. It was now early evening. The sun was low in the sky and the men were being eaten alive by midge flies. These miniscule flying pests didn't seem to bother the highland troops but the Franco-Irish troops detested them. Private O'Donnell moaned that he was being eaten alive to which his red-haired Sergeant answered, "They won't get much meat out of you lad."

The men laughed aloud, including Cameron, who spat out the water he had been drinking, in fits of laughter. A trooper of Fitz-James' arrived asking Cameron to attend yet another council of war. "Oh great" thought Cameron "more pointless arguing and more ridiculous decisions." Cameron made his way to the council room again.

This time the council of war did not last very long. A patrol had brought back news that Cumberland's army had stayed at Nairn and that it was the Duke of Cumberland's 25th birthday. It was proposed that the army march the twelve miles to Nairn by night and then take the government troops by surprise before dawn. It was hoped the Hanoverian troops would be drunk from celebrating their commander's birthday and would be easily routed. Lord George Murray again voiced his concerns about how hungry and under supplied the men were, some having as little as two rounds of ammunition per man and still no carts had arrived from Inverness with food. He agreed to the attack though. Cameron could tell Murray only agreed as it would theoretically avoid fighting on the wholly unsuitable ground of Drummossie moor. The night attack plan was soon unanimously approved and the Officers returned to their frustrated hungry men to tell them the 'good' news.

The news was greeted with mixed reactions by Cameron's men. Though professional soldiers they were not as used to the highland terrain as their Scots comrades and would find it difficult to keep up, especially in the dark. Moreover, the army couldn't take the most direct route to Nairn as they would stand too great a chance of being spotted, which could either lead to the enemy being in position waiting for them when they arrived or worse still, the Jacobites being counter attacked while out in the open strung out on the march, so the army had to take a less direct cross country route, almost twice as far. They did however, also know how short the clan regiments were on ammunition and Cameron remembered the success they had achieved at Prestonpans thanks to appearing unexpectedly through the morning mist near the enemy's position and falling upon them with cold steel where they were least expected.. With any luck this bold plan might just win them the war. It had to be done properly and professionally though, thought Cameron, and he was struggling to remember the last time this army had done anything professionally.

It was decided that the army should begin its night march at eight o'clock that evening. Even allowing for the extra distance the army would have to cover in avoiding the most direct route they should still arrive in plenty of time to give their government opponents a wholly nasty surprise at dawn.

The army set off in two separate columns. Lord George Murray led the clan units in the first column while the duke of Perth led the second column which was made up of the lowland units, the Royal Ecossaise and Cameron's Irish brigade. The Prince himself was in between the two columns with his life guards and the now exhausted men and horses of Fitz-James'. A company of some thirty men of clan MacIntosh acted as scouts as they were indigenous to the area and knew it well.

Officers' call before they departed had been brief, to say the least. Cameron was merely told that his men, along with the lowland regiments and the Royals, would be acting as a kind of anvil in marching directly towards Cumberland's army and attacking from the north while the hammer that was the clan units were to cross the river Nairn when about three miles from Cumberland's camp before re-crossing and taking the Hanoverians in the flank and rear. In theory the plan was plausible, mused Cameron and McDermott as they trudged through the quickly darkening highland landscape, still swatting the odd midge.

After a few hours of trudging across the pitch black uneven landscape it became obvious that a huge gap had opened up between Murray's highland column and the second column which included Cameron's men. The terrain was fine for nimble footed highlanders used to such hardship, especially since many had thrown away their targes so that they could march quicker, but things weren't so good for the second column. Cameron and his men along with the Royals simply weren't used to marching in formation over such rough, unpredictable and inhospitable terrain, especially in the pitch black of night.

The lowland regiments weren't doing much better in keeping up. Soon Cameron and his men passed clansmen from the lead column who had stopped through utter exhaustion. Even the threats of their Officers with levelled pistols and drawn swords weren't enough to make them march on.

An orderly from Murray arrived and told Cameron that the lead column had halted for a short time to allow the rest of the army to catch up but then a second orderly arrived, this time from the Prince himself telling the second column to halt.

Cameron and his men, along with the Royals, were by far the best troops in the Jacobite army but it was their unfamiliarity with such terrain in the dark that was compromising the whole attack. With no further orders coming from anyone they soon resumed their march but now it seemed that time was beginning to take the side of their enemies.

At around two O'clock that morning an orderly brought yet more orders to Cameron and the second column bearing the news they had all been dreading. The lead column hadn't even got within two miles of Cumberland's camp at Nairn before they heard the battalion drums beating and trumpets sounding. Whether or not Cumberland's men were aware of the approach of their enemies was still unclear but what was painfully clear to everyone in the Jacobite army now was that any chance of surprise was gone and they were now in very real danger of being caught strung out on the march by a numerically superior foe.

The order was relayed back to the men to turn around and head back to Culloden. Now they could add exhaustion to hunger, lack of ammunition, lack of decent gunners and lack of cavalry to their quickly diminishing chances of survival, let alone victory.

Cameron's order to about face was greeted with moans and grumbles by his men, though they quickly complied and started the long demoralising march back to Culloden. Cameron felt bad that it had been the slow progress of his unit over the unfamiliar terrain that had contributed into turning the night attack into a farce of the highest order. McDermott and Cameron agreed that the night attack plan had been folly but also that they had had little real alternative. By around six am the exhausted starving Jacobite army arrived back at Drummossie moor and threw themselves down to grab whatever sleep they could. Many clansmen wandered off in search of food as the carts STILL hadn't arrived from Inverness with the much needed supplies. Cameron drank some water and decided to get some sleep as no doubt that Hanoverian army was now fully aware of their enemy's abortive night attack and would be keen to close with the exhausted rebels and finish them off once and for all. Cameron felt himself begin to drift off to sleep. He had been sleeping for what seemed like only a few moments when he and most of his men were awoken by a cannon shot from their own artillery. The enemy was in sight!

CHAPTER NINETEEN

BEATING DRUMS

All around Culloden house and the side of Drummossie moor occupied by the Jacobites, men ran hurriedly towards the positions they had occupied the previous day, buckling on equipment, shouting to comrades and peering into the distance where what seemed like a long red serpent was emerging.

The Hanoverian army was obviously fully aware of the abortive attempt to surprise them the previous evening and was now closing in to finish off their exhausted starving enemy.

Cameron took brief orders from Brigadier Stapleton and read the orders of the day. All they stipulated was that no man was to strip or plunder enemy bodies until the battle was over, over-confidence that would have made Jack laugh had its nature not been so deluded.

Looking around, Cameron could see that although the army was deployed in the same manner in which it had been yesterday, there seemed to be far fewer men in the ranks. Many of the troops had wandered off in search of food and would obviously not be coming in back in time to fight the approaching Hanoverians. Nor had McPherson's men and the other absent clan units arrived other than a small party of MacDonalds so now, exhausted, starving and short on cavalry, artillery and manpower, they would face the full might of King George II's army.

Over on the left flank, the MacDonalds were in bad humour as they hadn't been given their traditional place on the right flank, an honour belonging to them since the days of King *Robert Bruce*. They had voluntarily relinquished this right on a number of occasions during *Montrose's* wars a century earlier but this time they had not been consulted and they were in a foul mood. In the rear Cameron could see the one hundred and fifty horses of Fitz-James' and the Life Guards cropping grass, a sure sign that it was not only men who were starving and exhausted from their fruitless night march. Cameron and his men knew from warfare on the continent that a heavy burden would fall on these horsemen should things start to go badly for the army. And the aforementioned horsemen and their mounts were in no fit state either physically or psychologically to compete with their far more numerically superior Hanoverian counterparts. Anything the Jacobite cavalry could do today would be at best, foolhardy and at worst, suicidal.

Private O'Donnell moaned aloud yet again to his Sergeant.

"God help us if they break our attack sir, their horse will cut us to pieces."

O'Donnell was right, thought Cameron, but he daren't let the men know it. Cameron turned to McDermott and asked quietly "well my friend, what think you of our chances?" McDermott replied.

"Well sir, we're outnumbered and outgunned and our horse might as well not be here. Our only chance is if these fierce highland devils can scatter the enemy again with their ferocious onslaught".

Cameron knew this too. They did have a chance, albeit a slim one, and it hinged on the fearsome highland charge by the clan units breaking the Hanoverian lines just as it had done at Prestonpans and Falkirk. By now the Hanoverian lines were less than two miles away, edging towards the Jacobite lines like a scarlet snake, ten thousand men strong. Cameron took in a deep breath, thought of his beloved Mary, of Caldwell, of Edinburgh and of the coming fight.

"God and King James" he said softly to himself.

When the distant Hanoverian army got to within two miles of the Jacobite lines Cameron saw them deploy into line of battle. They did this smoothly and effortlessly with the manner of men who seemed to have done this a hundred times before. Wind and sleet blew into the faces of the exhausted Jacobite army, adding one more iota of misery to their already seemingly desperate plight.

Cameron was elated to see from the enemy's flags that the extreme left of their line, facing the Jacobite right under Lord George Murray, was anchored by two regiments of infantry, Barrell's and Munro's. These regiments, like their comrades in the rest of the Hanoverian line, wore scarlet coats and tricorn hats or mitre caps.

These were far more formidable than the raw troops the Jacobites had faced at Prestonpans seven months earlier. Barrell's and Munro's were also however, two of the government regiments who had ran like a flock of frightened sheep from the fearsome Jacobite charge at Falkirk just over two months earlier. Now Cameron knew they had a chance. If the clans' initial advance could break these two cowardly regiments they would be able to roll up the entire Hanoverian line and put them to flight.

Barrell's and Munro's held the extreme left of the government front line, with Campbell's 21st, Price's 14th, Cholmondleys 34th border regiment and the Hanoverians' own Royal Scots regiment holding the extreme right.

Cameron and Stapleton, who had stopped by to check his men, noted the sad irony that all but one regiment of foot in the Hanoverian front line was Scots raised, the exception being Price's who hailed from West Yorkshire. Beyond Barrell's and Munro's on the extreme left, the flank was held by Lord Mark Kerr's dragoons, another Scottish unit. In between the front rank battalions were Colonel Belford's artillery in the form of ten three pounders placed in pairs between the battalions of foot soldiers. Cameron surveyed the enemy's dispositions through a looking glass borrowed from Stapleton.

Six battalions of foot made up the government second line, from left to right Sempill's, Wolfe's, Blighs, Conway's, Fleming's and Howard's. All but one of these regiments was raised in England.

The third line had only three battalions of foot, Blakeneys's, an Irish raised regiment, Battereau's 62nd and Pulteney's 13th. To the right and rear of this line Cameron could see were two cavalry formations, Cobhams dragoons and an unknown body of what looked like irregular cavalry. Cameron knew there was a good chance that this unit was the Duke of Kingston's light horse, a volunteer unit raised specifically to crush the rebellion, and he knew his accursed brother Callum was an officer over on the other side in that unit. Would he meet him today? Cameron didn't want to think about that right now, he had his own men to worry about.

Sergeant McDermott noted activity in the walled enclosure to the right of the Jacobite line and the men could hear pipes coming from that area. The Campbell militia. In force this time rather than the small party dealt with by Cameron and his Irish company earlier.

Cameron and McDermott had another brief discussion about the coming battle as the government battalions wheeled into place, now a mere four hundred yards from their Jacobite adversaries. Both men knew that most British regulars could fire two shots a minute. Cameron's men and the Royals to their right could manage three but that took training and discipline. Two volleys from the government line would not be enough to stop the advancing clans reaching the government lines in sufficient numbers to put them to flight once more. The government soldiers had barely managed one volley before turning tail and running at Prestonpans, while Falkirk had seen a similar outcome, though it had taken the intervention of the Irish brigade to tip the balance on one flank where the government troops had put up more of a stiff fight. Still, mused Cameron and McDermott, if the clans in the front line weren't subjected to too much artillery fire and the government troops fired even only two volleys they just might be victorious again. Those were big IF's though.

Now the pipes of the Jacobite army skirled across the moor in reply to the battalion drums of the Hanoverians. Looking around Cameron could see that this wasn't just two armies, two political groups and two royal houses facing each other. This was going to be a battle of the old world versus the new. On the one side, the mix and match quasi feudal Jacobite highlanders led by their chiefs and some carrying ancient weapons, supplemented by effective lowland units and superb French regulars, on the other side a scarlet coated modern war machine armed to the teeth with *brown bess* muskets, bayonets, cavalry and artillery. The cataclysmic encounter was at hand. And this was going to be very different from Fontenoy. VERY different.

Cameron fingered the razor sharp blade of his broadsword and gazed at the enemy across the field, wondering if he would meet his brother today. A Hanoverian Officer on horseback rode out to in between the two armies apparently checking the Jacobites' dispositions. No-one on the Jacobite side bothered firing at him. Suddenly Cameron saw a Jacobite highlander lope across to the Hanoverian lines and throw down his weapons, apparently making himself a prisoner. When the man was being led to the rear Cameron saw the man wrench a musket from a nearby soldier and turn it on Cumberland, but the man's guards shot him then beat him to death with musket butts. The enemy's commander seemed unharmed. The battle had claimed it's first casualty. Then Cameron heard a cannon shot...

CHAPTER TWENTY

THE DANCE BEGINS

To the surprise of almost everyone on the moor the first cannon shot came from the Jacobite guns, not the Royal Artillery. The shot sailed harmlessly over the heads of the Hanoverian front lines and came thumping down in the rear, slicing a poor unfortunate soldier of Pulteney's in half, splattering brains and entrails everywhere. Cameron prayed that the inexperienced men manning the Jacobite guns would improve on that with all haste. The next noise he heard came from four hundred yards away, the Royal Artillery had opened fire.

Cameron knew that an artillery duel was the standard first phase of any civilized continental battle, indeed the Duke of Cumberland had been known to say in Flanders that a battle without a cannonade was 'like a dance without music'.

However this was the first time the Jacobites had faced properly supplied artillery manned by trained gunners. At Prestonpans the government guns had been fired by one sole naval gunner after his comrades had ran away, while at Falkirk neither side had employed artillery, the Jacobites as all their guns were at Stirling Castle helping with the pointless siege while the Hanoverians had been unable to deploy sufficient artillery because of the weather. Now it was different. The ten Hanoverian three pounders pumped shots into the Jacobite front ranks at a rate of around one shot per minute, and every shot took effect, killing and maiming many of the Jacobites' best front line shock troops, who weren't helped by their officers ridiculous shouts of "close up close up" to fill the gaps left by the round shot.

In contrast Cameron could see the Jacobite gunnery having no effect, its shots were going high over their enemies' heads and landing harmlessly in the rear, though they did manage to take off a battalion horse's head. The Jacobite guns themselves soon became targets for the royal artillery and after ten minutes not a single shot was to be heard from the Jacobite artillery, most of the improvised gunners being smashed to bits with their poorly supplied pieces.

Cameron had never seen such a one sided artillery duel. It was obvious that the clans had to use their one but devastating tactic, the charge, as soon as possible otherwise the Hanoverians would win this battle with their artillery alone. Why didn't the clans advance? Looking to the rear Cameron could see that the vantage point chosen by the Prince and his advisors was a poor one, and the smoke from the uneven artillery duel only made that worse. Did the Prince, assuming battlefield command for the first time, know the effect the enemy guns were having on his best troops? Surely they had to advance soon. No order to attack came and for a further fifteen minutes the government guns pounded away with impunity at the thinning Jacobite front line.

"Those bastards will be loving this" moaned Private O'Donnell, "it's like punching a man who has his hands tied" he grumbled, referring to the fact that the Jacobite guns were silenced while the Hanoverian artillery pounded on.

"I'll punch you if you don't stop your moaning" answered Private McHardy, which raised a giggle from the Irish brigade. Private McHardy was just as frustrated as everyone else in the Jacobite army, it was no good being the best shot in the brigade if you were out of range of the enemy.

Suddenly a cannonball bounced over the heads of the Jacobite front line and landed among the Royal Ecossaise, killing two men and taking off another's leg.

More cannonballs smashed into the Jacobite second line and now Cameron was sure Cumberland's artillery was concentrating on thinning the Jacobite reserve as well as the front line troops. Privates Mountcashel and Sarsfield of Cameron's unit were killed by the same ball that even bounced on and killed an unhorsed cavalryman of Baggot's hussars in the third line. Surely the clans would attack now, this bombardment had been going on for almost half an hour. Cameron did the maths in his head, ten guns, one shot per minute per gun meant that as many as three hundred cannon balls had smashed into the Jacobite lines, with little or no reply.

McHardy asked Cameron "why don't they attack sir?".

Cameron simply answered by looking at the carnage around him and replying "would you if your guns alone would do the job?"

"Then why aren't we attacking?" continued McHardy, "this makes no sense at all, charging worked at Fontenoy, and on the last two occasions these devils faced the British."

Cameron strode over to the Private about to remind him just who was in command of the brigade when they all heard a colossal roar coming from the front and right of their own line. The clans had finally charged!

CHAPTER TWENTY-ONE

CLAYMORE

The order to attack had been delayed for two reasons. Firstly, the Jacobite commanders wanted to wait as long as possible for as many of their absent troops to return to the line as possible, not just McPherson's elite regiment but the hundreds of starving men who had wandered off desperate for something to fill their bellies. Secondly, the soldier carrying the order to the front line to attack had his head taken off by a cannonball en route, further delaying the advance and giving the Royal Artillery a precious extra few moments to plough more shots into the now sorely depleted Jacobite ranks. Nevertheless, whether it was from a renewed order, frustration about being decimated without being able to reply or just pure blood lust, the clans in the front line surged forward across Drummossie Moor towards their scarlet-coated enemies.

The Gaelic war cries of the clans filled the air as they rushed towards the Hanoverian lines. The Hanoverian troops stood silent and motionless, like a wall of scarlet and white, waiting for orders.

Cameron had to roar an order to halt to his men as half of them tried to follow the MacDonalds in front of them into the attack but with Sergeant McDermott's help he managed to get them back into line.

"*Cuimnidh ar Luimneach agus ar Feall na Sasanach*" roared Cameron, relishing being in command of these fearsome men.

Cameron and his men looked on as a tartan tidal wave swept across the moor towards the scarlet-coated ranks at the far end. Cameron conceded to McDermott that he had never seen such a terrifying site, McDermott agreed.

"Thank god it's not us they're charging"

It seemed that it was a completely fresh highland army who charged the Hanoverians. Gone were all signs of starvation. Gone were all signs of fatigue. The icy cold highland wind that swept the moor and blew sleet into their faces did nothing to dent the speed of their ferocious onslaught. All the while, as the clans charged, the Hanoverian cannon continued thumping round shot into their ranks, but still they advanced.

Clansmen collapsed screaming, having lost arms or legs as the balls that had maimed them bounced on to cause further carnage in the ranks behind them. Still the heroic Celtic warriors bore down on the

Hanoverian foot and guns. When the clans reached two hundred yards the Royal Artillery's bombardiers switched to grape shot, ramming large musket balls and old iron into the muzzle instead of solid shot. The effect at short range was devastating. *Grape shot* turned the three pounder cannons into giant shotguns, spewing red hot iron and musket balls that tore horrendous gaps in the ranks of the tartan mob advancing towards them and causing horrific injuries. Whole companies of clansmen disappeared. But still their remaining comrades charged.

Cameron was struggling to see through the smoke and sleet but he could see that a hidden undulation in the ground had caused the centre of the Jacobite front line to veer off to their right so that they formed a huge unwieldy mob intermingled with their own right wing. And Cameron could see that the mob was bearing down on the two regiments on the extreme left of the government line, Barrell's and Munro's, the two regiments who had ran from the clans at Falkirk only a couple of months earlier. Cameron watched in awe. As the clans reached one hundred and fifty yards range the muskets of the Hanoverian infantry were levelled at them ready to deliver a devastating hail of lead. "Two rounds sir" said McDermott confidently," the English will manage two rounds then our lads will have them".

Cameron knew his Sergeant was right. It was unheard of for British troops to fire more than twice a minute. CRASH. The first volley of musket fire rang out from the left of the Hanoverian line taking down the leading ranks of the charging clans who were now only one hundred yards away, CRASH the second volley was delivered, the Hanoverians firing by platoons with devastating effect, but Cameron saw that any second now the clans would smash the Hanoverian line like a hammer breaking glass. It was all about hand to hand fighting now, bayonets against swords and Lochaber axes, a contest the clans would surely win easily, or so Cameron thought. CRASH.

CHAPTER TWENTY-TWO

MAKE READY

The third and unexpected volley of platoon firing from the Hanoverian lines chilled Cameron's blood and gave him a sinking feeling in his stomach. The redcoats had obviously been practicing their reloading and firing while they were at Aberdeen to devastating effect. And those extra eight hundred or so musket balls made all the difference. The extra volley ensured that when the clans reached the government lines, they did so in insufficient numbers to completely rout the troops in front of them. Cameron told McDermott and his men to prepare for cavalry and the expected Hanoverian counter attack and the rest of the units in the Jacobite second line did the same. On the left, the MacDonald regiments, though disgruntled about being posted on what they saw as the wrong wing of the army, had began their advance but couldn't close with the redcoat infantry thanks to the ground being so boggy, something O'Sullivan should have noted. Here the men of Keppoch, Glengarry and Clanranald stood firing their muskets, roaring insults and even throwing stones at the Hanoverian troops to their front.

The Macdonalds were unwilling to advance, not because of the hail of musketry aimed at them or because they had been posted on the left wing, what stopped them was the appearance of a huge body of enemy cavalry on their exposed flank in the form of the Duke of Kingston's light horse. For a time it was stalemate on the Jacobite left. Over on the right the battle hung in the balance.

Despite everything, despite their hunger, fatigue and the intense bombardment they had been forced to endure, the Jacobite right and centre made it to the Hanoverian lines. Many of the clansmen had thrown away their targes on the abortive night march and in the confusion of the charge many of them had thrown away their firearms rather than fire their customary short range volley yet still they reached the bayonets of the Hanoverian lines. This time however, Barrell's and Munro's stood and fought like lions. This would indeed be no re run of the battle of Fontenoy or Falkirk.

In the ferocious hand to hand combat that ensued, the clans, against all odds, sent most of Barrell's and Munro's running back to form up on the flanks of their own second line, while those Hanoverian soldiers unable to run fought until they were cut down. No quarter was asked nor given at this stage. Scot fought Scot. Sword against Bayonet. Muskets and pistols fired at short range. It was carnage but somehow the clans were doing it again, against all odds. Beating the British army. Any minute now they would surely surge on to the second line and put them to flight as well. wheeeeeeeeeeeeeBANG.

Cameron looked across the field, his attention temporarily diverted from the plight of the MacDonalds to his front. He knew that sound. It was a *Coehorn mortar.* Why were the government troops using siege weapons at close range? Peering through the looking glass again Cameron saw that the mortar shells were falling, not among the highland clans who were bearing down on the government second line but they were exploding just behind the government second line. Cumberland was using mortars on his own men to stop them from running away!

The cowardly despicable actions of the Hanoverian commander proved to be a trump card if ever there was one. Unable to run from the highland onslaught the redcoats had no option but to stand and shoot as the clans rushed at them. The Hanoverian Royal Scots fusiliers formed up at a right angle to the second line while the survivors of Barrells and Munro's formed up on their other flank. While this was going on, Wolfe's regiment was sent to reinforce the Argyle militia in the walled enclosure who had peppered the Jacobite right's advance with flanking fire. This ensured that if the Jacobite right and centre retreated they would be subject to enfilade fire as well as fire from their rear.

Worse still for the Jacobites, Lord Mark Kerr's regiment of dragoons had been sent around the enclosure in an attempt to cut off any Jacobite retreat to *Ruthven barracks,* the Jacobites' pre arranged meeting place in event of defeat. The only thing that stood in the way of the Jacobite right being encircled was a deep sunken road and the seventy red-coated troopers of Fitz-James' horse who had dismounted and were using their carbines to defend it. Gordon's and Glenbucket's regiments were also sent to counter the threat to the right where they kept back the Argyle militia and elements of *Wolfe's* regiment, keeping the vital Ruthven road open.

CHAPTER TWENTY-THREE

COVERING THE REAR

As far as the Jacobite front line went, the battle was lost. The right and centre elements who braved the Hanoverian firestorm and smashed the first line now found themselves surrounded on three sides by redcoats who fired volley after volley into them at close range. It was a massacre. Vain attempts by Murray to bring up the second line came to nothing but it was Cumberland's bizarre and chilling decision to simply mortar his own men to prevent them from running that had sealed the Jacobites' fate. Slowly, the tartan torrent edged back across the moor, many men musketless, swordless and covered in blood, all the while blasted with musket fire from their rear by the victorious government troops and by Wolfe's men behind the walls to their left.

Fitz James' were forced to abandon the sunken road when they ran out of carbine ammunition and this gave new heart to Lord Mark Kerr's dragoons, now willing to brave the sunken road even though they had outnumbered the Jacobite horsemen by nine to one anyway. Some of Fitz-James' were sent with Lord Elcho's Life Guards to escort the Prince from the field. The Prince was sobbing uncontrollably fearing that he had seen the last hopes of his dynasty regaining their rightful throne smashed forever, but sympathy was in short supply, Lord Elcho screaming after him "run you cowardly Italian".

The remaining forty Jacobite horse, led by Lord Strathallan, made one last attempt to hold the government horse now pouring out in pursuit of the routed clans by making a near suicidal charge but their action was at best a delaying one and all their horses were soon riderless, Lord Strathallan avoiding the scaffold by dying in battle and taking a multitude of enemies with him.

Cameron surveyed the scene of the utter carnage around him. The Irish Brigade and the Royal Ecossaise were as yet unengaged and had only suffered minimal casualties in the one sided bombardment. The other second line units had been sent to cover the threat to the army's right but were now retreating in reasonable order towards Ruthven.

Cameron had seen his namesake clan and their allies come so close to breaking the Hanoverian lines once again. He had seen the ruthless tactics employed by Cumberland to prevent his men from running away and he had seen the routed Jacobite right and centre fall back battered and decimated most of them along the Ruthven road. He had also seen the Prince and his entourage make a sharp exit but now Jack Cameron had more pressing matters on his hands.

The MacDonalds had been unable or unwilling to advance and they now had two, not one, bodies of Hanoverian horse on their flank. Cameron remembered what the cavalry had done to his namesake clansmen back at Braemuir when the horsemen had taken the unprotected clansmen in the open. He was damned if he was going to let that happen to the MacDonald clans too. As the routed MacDonalds streamed through his men towards the rear, Cameron decided the best thing to do was to hold the Inverness road as long as he could to allow as many men as possible to escape. Cameron and his men opened their ranks to let the fleeing clansmen through giving them a warm cheer as they did so. By now only the Irish brigade and the Royal Ecossaise were still capable of fighting coherently. The moor to their front and right was a sickening mess of corpses, wounded and dying men, weapons, horses, flags and plaids. There weren't very many enemy corpses.

Cameron could see that the battle was lost, but also that his work and that of his professional soldiers was just about to begin. Resolved to hold the Inverness road, the Irish brigade and the Royals formed double ranks and waited. The rest of what was left of the Jacobite army was pouring in the other direction towards the pre arranged assembly point at Ruthven barracks in Badenoch, only a few miles away. Brigadier Stapleton and Cameron with their respective units reformed their lines after the MacDonalds had fled through. Through the thick smoke they heard the thunder of the hooves of massed cavalry bearing down upon them. Cameron roared to his men to make ready as the large body of scarlet coated enemy cavalry that had been set to pursue clan Donald changed direction and headed straight for them. They had to hold their fire until the Hanoverian horse were within near point blank range or their volley would not have suitable effect and they could be ridden down. They had to hold.

The next sound Cameron heard was a dull moan as Brigadier Stapleton went down wounded. He was shot in the chest and was carried to the rear of the line by two soldiers of the Royal Ecossaise. This left Cameron in command of both the Irish brigade and the Royals, by now further reduced but still numbering some four hundred men. As the first ranks of Hanoverian cavalry appeared out of the thick smoke Cameron roared the command "FIRE" and four hundred musket balls slammed into the front rank of the enemy horse, killing some and temporarily making the others halt and resort to pistols and carbines.

"Reload" roared Cameron, but most of his men had already began that process. A substantial body of Hanoverian horse bypassed the Irish brigade's line and threatened to encircle them but Cameron quickly had the Royal's first battalion turn to their right and rear and had their young Lieutenant direct volleys that for the time being, nullified the threat of encirclement and kept the Inverness road open.

"Shoot at the bloody horses" growled McDermott to the Irish lads, knowing that they stood a better chance of hitting the target if they aimed low. The Hanoverian horse were soon joined by another regiment and their numbers began to tell on Cameron and his men. Cameron had his two units walking backwards towards the Inverness road firing murderous volleys as they went, keeping back Cobhams dragoons and the Nottinghamshire volunteers of Kingston's horse. It hadn't escaped Cameron's notice that his brother's regiment was attacking his own, he just had more pressing concerns, particularly his men's ammunition situation. McHardy shouted that he was down to eight rounds, and the battalion drums sounding from across the moor indicated that the Hanoverian foot were about to advance to take customary victorious possession of the ground previously occupied by the enemy. There was a brief respite while the Hanoverian horse reformed to try and once again charge these fearsome Scots and Irishmen who wore the uniforms of France.

Cameron started to think about his beloved Mary, if he was killed or taken prisoner she would be all on her own in the world. Jack also knew that his commission in his most Catholic majesty's army was worthless and he could not expect to be treated as a prisoner of war if captured, particularly if spotted by his brother. He was however, the acting commander of what was left of the Jacobite army on Drummossie moor. What was he to do? He couldn't abandon his men and leave them leaderless, even though the battle was clearly lost. He couldn't surrender yet either, as the Inverness road still had to be held for the Jacobite fugitives who had chosen that particular route. His decision was made for him when once again a huge body of Hanoverian horse charged his little battalion. Cameron decided they would fight until their ammunition was expended, but he was now denied the services of the Royals as they were forced to swing back to their left and exchange volleys with the Hanoverian Royal Scots, a sad irony of the battle if ever there was one.

"FIRE" roared Cameron and the Irish lads blasted another deadly hail of lead into the enemy horse, downing men and horses but this time the cavalry got in close, hacking away with sabres while Cameron's men defended themselves with bayonets. It was a fearsome struggle. A tall dragoon aimed a pistol at Cameron at point blank range but looked very confused when the weapon sparked but did not fire. Cameron wasted no time in skewering his mounted opponent with his own musket and bayonet before the trooper could reload. Turning instantly, Cameron saw another enemy trooper fall from the saddle beside him, shot by a blood soaked and wounded Private O'Donnell.

His musket firmly imbedded in the troopers' body, Jack drew the fearsome basket hilted broadsword given to him by his late friend Lieutenant Caldwell and drove it into the belly of a horse whose rider was fighting savagely with Private McHardy. The horse threw its stunned rider and a surprised but grateful McHardy duly finished the trooper off with his bayonet.

Sergeant McDermott was fighting equally heroically. His blood curdling Gaelic battle cries inspired the Irish brigade to hold the Hanoverian horse for much longer than they should have been able to, but in the end they could only realistically expect to fight for as long as they had cartridges to fire. The men were already pinching cartridges from dead and wounded comrades but the obvious thinning of their volleys was enough to persuade the Hanoverian cavalry and their supporting infantry to press home their final assault. Cameron could see that almost half of his combined command was dead or wounded and that the men were completely out of ammunition. McHardy dropped another enemy trooper with his last cartridge then grabbed Cameron's arm declaring "you're a dead man when they take us prisoner sir, you should go while you can. Go to your woman, for god's sake."

"I won't leave my lads like this," protested Cameron, but McHardy retorted.

"We'll be taken prisoner and exchanged later. You won't. The battle is lost sir, now go". It was the last thing McHardy ever said. Two carbine balls smashed into his skull splattering his brains all over Cameron's face. Stunned, Cameron seemed paralysed for a moment until through the thick smoke, which was making things very difficult for both sides, he saw a sight that chilled his blood and made him even more angry than he already was.

Out of the smoke charged his brother Callum. Straight towards him. Cameron raised the heavy broadsword and parried his brother's first blow then sliced off Callum's horses nose, making it throw its rider.

"For the love of god go sir" roared Sergeant McDermott. "Lieutenant Hogg of the Royals will look after us and make sure we get treated right, now go, and god go with you."

Cameron looked at the blue-coated Hogg who was reloading his pistol. Hogg nodded and agreed with McDermott. Cameron seized the bridle of the nearest enemy horse and, after stabbing its rider in the stomach, mounted the beast and made off along the Inverness road. He turned in the saddle just in time to see his brother run McDermott through with his sabre but he couldn't think about vengeance now. The last thing he saw as he gradually put hundreds then thousands of yards between himself and the battlefield was the Royals and his own men laying down their arms in surrender. They had fought like lions. Cameron felt proud to be part of such a noble Jacobite unit, even if they had ultimately been on the losing side today. He had emulated his grandfather's feats at Killiecrankie and the Boyne of some fifty six years ago and also the noble deeds of his own father in the risings of 1715 and 1719. Now all he cared about was getting to Elgin and Mary before the vengeful enemy did. The army might well fight on if enough of it reassembled at Ruthven but Jack Cameron, after seeing so many of his friends and comrades die in the last eight months, wanted to play no further part in this war.

CHAPTER TWENTY-FOUR

FLIGHT AND DELIGHT

He took a cross-country route, as he knew the Inverness-Elgin road would now be full of rampant Hanoverian cavalry looking for Jacobite fugitives to kill or capture, probably the former, he thought. How he hated his accursed brother. Jack wanted to kill him, but he knew that was unlikely now. He also knew that those men in his unit and the Royals who were not enlisted men in the French service prior to 1745 would be treated as traitors and rebels rather than prisoners of war, though he was confident that the majority of his former command would be treated humanely. His brother would no doubt deal with those unfortunate enough not to be in legitimate French service. His brother had effectively killed his unborn child, beaten his lover, caused the death of his friend and killed many of Jack's comrades in arms, including the fearsome Sergeant McDermott, but all Jack wanted now was to go and get Mary and try to get to one of the French ships that were appearing periodically up and down the northern coast of Scotland, to escape. He couldn't stay in Scotland now and risk transportation or worse. By early evening Jack was nearing Elgin, and by the look of things he was the first man from the battle to get there as everything seemed reasonably calm and normal ahead. The sun began to sink in the sky as he entered the town.

Several of Elgin's townsfolk came out to greet Jack, one in particular, a stout woman who introduced herself as Marjorie, surprisingly said in her coarse accent ' well since you've returned alone and without your musket I assume our Prince has been defeated?".

Surprised at this woman's uncanny knack for smelling the truth, Cameron merely nodded, an act that made all the women who had come to investigate his arrival gasp in horror and make the sign of the cross. "And what of the rest of the army, and our Prince?" enquired Marjorie further. Cameron dismounted and informed the terrified townsfolk
  "It lasted little more than an hour, the usurpers' men were too many and better equipped than us. Our charge was heroic but futile and we lost half our number, my men and I held the Inverness road for as long as we could to allow clan Donald to escape along it, the remnants of the rest of

the army headed towards Ruthven in rout. I know not what will become of the army now."

"You look exhausted and hungry" interrupted Marjorie "come and eat with us before those accursed English get here and take everything we have, Mary is desperate to see you."

Cameron was eager to see his love but aware that she was probably very ill after losing their child from the earlier beating she had received. He was to be shocked. Very shocked indeed.

As Jack and old Marjorie entered the house of Mary's late father, Jack was greeted by an amazing site. Rather than seeing his beautiful woman lying ill crying in bed she was sat up, her dress open, breast feeding a tiny baby! His baby! Jack Cameron's baby! Overjoyed at this he rushed over and embraced them both, tears running down his face, and that of his affianced.

His child, though very small, showed all signs of good health, commented Marjorie before leaving the room to give Jack and Mary some time alone.

"I'm so glad you're safe my love" said Mary.

"And I you" retorted Jack," and our child, I feared those Hanoverian scum had deprived me of you both."

The new little family embraced again before Mary said "It's a boy Jack. Our wee boy. I thought we might call him James."

This suggestion made Jack's heart swell with pride even more and he readily agreed to name their son after the rightful King of Scotland. He quickly explained to Mary how the battle had been lost, though she already knew the horrid fate of her male relatives and the town's men folk.

Their reunion was interrupted when they heard the unmistakable sound of horses hooves coming from out in the town square. Cameron grabbed his sword and made for the door, where he saw four blue-coated cavalrymen, one of whom was obviously badly wounded. One of the troopers saw Jack peering round the corner and cried out "identify yourself." Cameron realized from the blue coats that these were men of Lord Elcho's Life Guards, the Prince's personal bodyguard. Relieved at this, he approached them. The four men looked exhausted, and one was groaning from his wounds.

One trooper, a blood splattered crazed Irishman identified himself as Divers, and his tale confirmed what Jack had already instinctively known.

"The war is over for now Captain Cameron" said Divers, "we make for the west coast and hope to be picked up by French ships, our Prince seems to have made the same decision. Inverness is now in Cumberland's hands and the redcoats are butchering our wounded back on Drummossie moor, perhaps you would like to join us in our flight Captain?"

Knowing that escaping to France with his woman and newborn son was his only option, Cameron agreed to accompany the troopers on the condition that he could bring his new family with him, to which the troopers agreed.

"Come eat and drink with us before we depart" Cameron invited the troopers, but he was swiftly reprimanded by Divers who declared "we must leave NOW sir, there is a body of about forty enemy horse close on our tail, butchering everyone they come across, we must leave now."

"My woman and child will slow us down" resigned Cameron, "you must go, leave me a carbine and some cartridges so that I may defend my family."

They were interrupted by the wounded trooper who had dismounted and opened his tunic to reveal a ghastly musket ball wound to his abdomen.

The trooper said "I'm done for anyways my comrades, Why don't you all go now, leave me your carbines and pistols and I will slow the enemy to aid your escape" Cameron addressed this dying but hugely courageous man.

"And what is your name?"

"Lewis Caldwell sir, my older Brother was with Fitz James', I hear you and he were good friends."

Cameron saw the facial similarities between this young man and his old friend Caldwell who had turned traitor but ultimately redeemed himself. Even with four carbines and four pistols this wounded man would have no chance against a troop of bloodthirsty enemy horse. But Cameron and the other three troopers also knew he stood no chance of surviving more than a couple of hours anyway with such a wound, and the young Caldwell knew it too. Cameron and the four troopers shook hands before Jack headed back into the house to tell Mary to grab a few belongings and their son and be ready to leave.

As Divers helped Mary and wee James into the saddle of the young Caldwell's horse, Cameron and the other two men carried Caldwell upstairs to a high window, where they propped him up against the wall beside it, leaving him their firearms and cartridges, and some water.

Cameron then asked the two troopers to go and keep watch for the enemy, leaving himself and the young Caldwell alone.

"My family and I and your brave comrades owe you our lives" said Cameron.

The young Caldwell replied "I know what my brother was but I said nothing as he was still my brother, and I know he died to help you and your men escape, maybe I can do the same for you as he did Captain Cameron."

"Jack, please, call me Jack" replied Cameron.

"I also know your brother Callum fights for King George" continued Caldwell.

"He's no brother of mine" replied Cameron, "If he had half the courage or loyalty as you or your brother then perhaps I would see him as such, but he has not, and though it may make me a sinner, I wish my brother dead for what he has done."

Caldwell answered "the Officer leading our pursuers looked suspiciously like you Jack, I hope your wish comes true when they reach this town." Both men knew instinctively what that last statement meant. A final handshake was shared before Jack helped the wounded man load his eight weapons and headed down the stairs to set off with Mary, wee James and the other three Life Guards, west, as quickly as they could, soon Elgin was far behind them.

CHAPTER TWENTY-FIVE

REVENGE

Around thirty minutes later a troop of Hanoverian horse entered the town of Elgin once more. They trotted through cautiously before their officer ordered his men to murder all the town's inhabitants as this place was a 'cesspit of rebel dogs".

They were the last orders he ever gave.

A musket ball from a nearby house slammed into his genitals, quickly followed by another one into his belly. The officer slumped from his mount and fell onto the ground, screaming and gurgling in agony at the same time. Two further shots downed troopers beside him, then four pistol shots rang out in quick succession, killing another three troopers and killing a fourth trooper's horse from under him. Leaderless, the cavalry retreated from the town believing it to be heavily defended. They also left their officer, Callum Cameron, bleeding slowly to death in agony on the ground. It took him several hours to die. The townspeople just left him there, remembering the atrocities he had committed only a few days before. The young Caldwell was fast succumbing to his wounds and this was why he had missed with his last shot and only hit a trooper's horse. But he had done his final job heroically. He took one last look at the pathetic evil officer writhing on the cobbled stones before sipping his water and drifting into that eternal slumber, the permanent sleep called death, his dying words were a murmured expression of 'god and King James'. He died of his wounds, so that when the Hanoverians arrived in greater force they found only one enemy corpse and didn't even get the satisfaction of finishing him off. They had expected to find a whole Jacobite regiment.

Jack Cameron and his new family, along with the three remaining Life Guards, made good their escape, though, like their Prince, it was an escape filled with intrigue and danger. They were relieved to finally board a French frigate near loch Shiel, and even more relieved when the frigate's captain evaded a Royal Navy squadron to land them all safely at the French port of Brest. It had been an adventure, quite an adventure, but now Jack was to begin a new adventure, one of sacred marriage and of parenthood, though his grief for the Caldwell brothers and all his other comrades who had fallen so far from their homes fighting for the rightful

King would be with him forever, as would his sympathy for the highlands, now almost defenceless against a vengeful Hanoverian regime that was determined to snuff out Jacobitism once and for all. Scotland, and indeed Britain, would never be the same again.

A sullen, dejected Cameron leaves the battlefield intent on finding Mary.

Lieutenant Caldwell of Fitz-James' orders a search for Cameron to be mounted.

The evil William Campbell

The defeated, dejected clans reassemble at Ruthven, only to be later disbanded as an army.

The outnumbered Irish Brigade hold back the Hanoverian tide, allowing the rest of the army to escape.

An Irish soldier ignores the hail of English lead to carefully pick his target.

Jack and the Irish Brigade wait patiently in line for the inevitable Hanoverian counter attack.

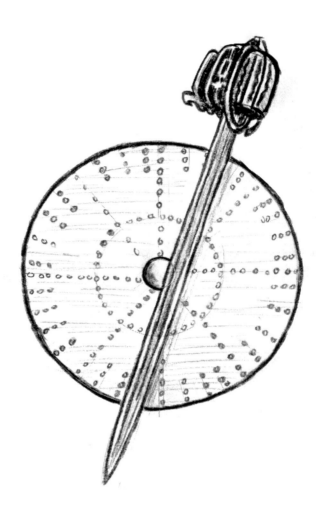

A basket hilted broadsword and targe, weapons carried by the elite among the Jacobite highland units.

Jack Cameron

Alasdair Cameron makes his final charge.

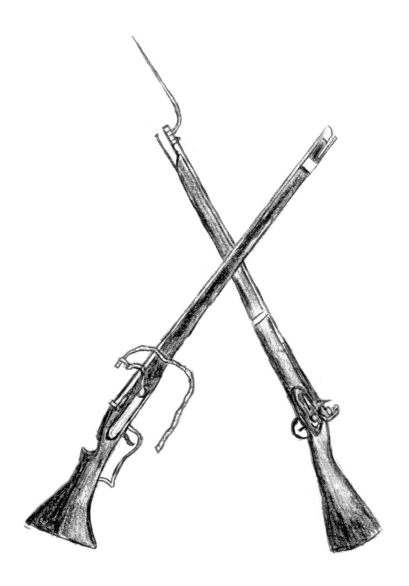

A flintlock musket complete with socket bayonet and an older matchlock musket.

Private O'Donnell of the Irish Brigade in full uniform with his weapons.

Author's notes, views, and Historical corrections

To the best of my knowledge, there was no officer named Jack Cameron serving in the Franco-Scottish-Irish units in the Jacobite army, though the background I created for him is typical of such men and their ancestors or descendants who left Scotland or Ireland from the 1690's until the French revolution of 1789 to enlist in the service of Catholic France, who, for most of the time, sponsored and supported the rightful Kings of England and Scotland in exile, the Stuarts, though the French only provided this support when it suited them.

The same goes for most of the Jacobite soldiers I have mentioned, the lads in the Irish company are named after friends of mine, as is trooper Divers of the Prince's Life Guard. The names of regiments and commanding officers on both sides are accurate however, as is the depiction of the battle of Culloden and the abortive night march to Nairn which preceded it.

Captain Cameron's unit, a company or picquet of Dillon's regiment, did exist and, with the other two Irish companies, along with the Franco Scottish exiles regiment the Royal Ecossaise (Royal Scots) they covered the retreat of the routed clans who poured along the Inverness road when their infamous 'highland charge' had been repulsed. These regular units, though few in number, held back the Hanoverians long enough for what was left of the Jacobite army to make it's escape. Those who made for the pre arranged assembly point at Ruthven barracks arrived only to be disbanded and given the order "every man for himself for now" by the Prince. Those Jacobites who ran along the Inverness road weren't so fortunate and government cavalry, who also took great delight in slaughtering any hapless civilians they encountered along the way, cut many of them down.

I 'borrowed' the men burnt to death in the barn part from a story relating to the battle of Culloden itself, though no archaeological evidence of this atrocity has even been found, despite several attempts. There was a skirmish in Elgin between the Jacobite Irish Brigade redcoats and a rabble of pro government militia in 1746 not long before Culloden and the 'redcoats' were successful in driving the pro Hanoverian clans out of the town using their superior firepower.

It is a fact that a French musket's calibre was smaller than that of British muskets, which gave a limited advantage to the British, as they could still fit the smaller French balls into their weapons and fire them in case of emergency, thought it made them wildly inaccurate, whereas French muskets were of smaller caliber meaning British ammo simply wouldn't fit down the muzzle. This was a major problem for the Jacobites at Aughrim in 1691 when they couldn't use the vast stores of ammunition captured from the Williamites in a raid by Patrick Sarsfield a few weeks earlier. Cameron and his men had to destroy it in the story, as they would have had to do so in reality.

Forget the romantic myth of highland clansman armed with sword and shield fighting government redcoats armed with musket and bayonet. Yes, they often fought with crude edged weapons but government troops recovered over fifteen hundred French muskets from the Culloden battlefield, and only one hundred and seventy broadswords, that tells you how the Jacobite army at Culloden was armed. Two thousand Jacobite soldiers were killed, wounded or captured in the hour long battle, government losses were given as a mere fifty men killed but recent geophysical studies on the government burial pit suggest that figure to be nearer three hundred. Still an awfully one sided affair. There is similar evidence that Cumberland dropped mortar shells to the rear of his own men, which explains why they didn't run from the clans like they usually did. Another myth about Cumberland teaching his men a special bayonet drill, where each soldier attacked the clansman to his right's unprotected shield-less side rather than the man directly to his front, is usually overstated and in practice nigh on impossible to co ordinate, but this training would at least have taught his men to trust each other more.

Much is made of the twenty to thirty minute bombardment the Jacobites faced before advancing, but the cannon fired solid shot, not exploding shells, and it's impossible that more than three hundred cannon balls struck the Jacobite lines, and with such wet ground not all of these balls would have bounced. The Jacobite army was ripped apart by disciplined musket fire and close range grape shot, not by solid cannon balls.

It's a well known fact that Jacobite wounded were butchered where they lay on the field, one Hanoverian officer remarking that his men looked like 'so many butchers' as they splashed around in blood and finished off wounded Jacobite troops with their new fangled socket Bayonets, to save ammunition. Many wounded clansmen were even clubbed to death or simply left out to die of exposure. The 'Butcher' tag was soon to become associated with the Hanoverian commander, William Augustus, Duke of Cumberland and second son of George II. Prince Charles was in fact his cousin.

Though atrocities were undoubtedly committed by the government troops after the battle, it is worth remembering that Cumberland's orders after the battle included the phrase "Officers and men will note that the enemy's orders today were to give us no quarter", though some scholars think that this had been added to the end of a captured Jacobite order. Cumberland, though previously an average general, can be partly excused in that he was defending what he believed to be his father's rightful crown and to secure it, and prevent a feared large scale French landing in support of the rising, he had to deal with the Jacobites ruthlessly.

Prince Charles has often been accused of cowardice, as echoed by Lord Elcho's statement towards the end of the battle, and of deserting his loyal followers, but this seems a little harsh. When what was left of his army reassembled at Ruthven they had lost all their baggage and artillery. Their best regular troops, the Irish brigade and the Royal Ecossaise, had lost half their number during the battle and the rest had been taken prisoner. They had also lost most of their best highland units to the grapeshot and muskets of the Hanoverians, and their small cavalry force, save the tiny squadron who escorted the Prince from the battlefield, had been completely destroyed. Furthermore, with Inverness now in government hands, the Jacobites had no access to the meal store from which they were paying and feeding their men. Though McPherson of Cluny's elite regiment and a few other units who hadn't made it back in time for the battle did arrive at Ruthven, they were only an extra thousand or so men who had to be fed and given ammunition, and there was neither food nor ammunition for them. Charles seems to have lost interest in his army as soon as it lost all resemblance of being a conventional force and he wisely decided to return to France to petition King Louis for more help.

History, at least in the earlier days, is written by the winners though and the Prince has since been tainted with a reputation as having simply ran away and abandoned his men. The same falsehood was applied to his Grandfather after the battle of the Boyne in 1690 (which was a successful Jacobite rearguard action rather than the crushing Williamite victory of myth, the Williamite war was decided a year later at Aughrim, and then only by armistice, not Williamite victory). Again in that instance, James left Ireland, not in flight, but to beseech his ally Louis XIV to invade

England while the Williamite army was tied down in Ireland. The British army under John Churchill (later the Duke of Marlborough) had not been taken to Ireland as William of Orange didn't trust their loyalty, and they would have sided with James had he landed in England, according to many reliable sources.

The story of James getting back to Dublin after the Boyne to complain about his Irish troops running away only to be told "it is you sir who has won the race", implying that he reached Dublin before his army, is a barefaced lie. James didn't enter Dublin until ten pm that evening as he had been overseeing the organized withdrawal of his army. The lady to whom the "you have won the race" quote is attributed to, Lady Tyrconnell, was in Limerick at the time, not Dublin.

Louis XIV wanted the Williamite army tied down in Ireland for as long as possible though, so there was no invasion of England, even though at the time the French had heavy naval superiority. The longer the Irish war dragged on, the better the chances of France gaining the upper hand in the wider continental struggle.

The same situation explains both Charles' departure to France after Culloden and the half hearted attempts to aid his army by the French. The civil war in Scotland had seen nearly twenty battalions of British troops rushed back home from Flanders where they had been fighting the French. This explains why the promised French invasion in support of the rising never materialized, and why barely two thousand 'French' troops were sent to aid the Jacobites (about 30% of whom were intercepted by the Royal navy en route). The French aided the Jacobites so as to gain an advantage on the continent and divert British troops, not out of any great love for the Stuarts, though many French aristocrats and high ranking officers had Jacobite sympathies on a personal level.

As for the actual soldiers of the 'French' units sent to Scotland though, they fought like lions and must have been frustrated at being there in such small numbers. With a force of three of four thousand regulars behind them, the Scottish Jacobites might well have triumphed, though it is difficult to assess how the people of England would have welcomed a new King who arrived with an army supplied by their arch enemy. Then again, Londoners have always been fans of the winning side and had no such problems accepting William III's usurping of the throne in 1688 when he arrived with a largely foreign force at his back, supplemented by traitors and defectors like Churchill and Mackay.

Contrary to popular myth, the Jacobites continued fighting after 1746, most notably under Cameron of Locheil, still receiving the odd shipment of gold and arms from France and carrying on a guerrilla style war, albeit on a very small scale, until at least 1753. During the years that followed, Prince Charles significantly changed his political stance and converted to Anglicanism in an attempt to appeal more to protestants back in Britain. The last great act of the Jacobite crisis was the little known naval battle of Quiberon bay in 1759. Charles armed with his new manifesto for radical reform and his new Anglican religion, the entire Irish brigade and thousands of French regulars and Scots exiles, set out to invade England, though this was, as usual, more to do with Britain's war with France (the Seven Years war) than with France helping their Stuart friends. France wanted a friendly monarch on the British throne, and who can blame Charles for wanting one last throw of the dice. Ultimately though, the invasion fleet was defeated easily by the Royal Navy under Admiral Hawke at Quiberon bay and with that defeat came the end of the Jacobite cause as a political movement, though it has survived ever since as a romantic notion.

The Irish brigade of France were among the best units in the French army and fought valiantly for the Bourbons all over the world, becoming a constant thorn in Britain's side. Referring to the harsh anti Catholic penal laws imposed on the Irish after the English broke the treaty of Limerick of 1691, king George II was quoted as saying

"I curse these harsh laws that deprive my armies of such valiant men".

The red coated Irish brigade served France in their red coats until the revolution in 1789, when most of their officers and men returned home rather than serve the new regime. It is no coincidence that within only nine years of them returning home there was a serious uprising against British rule in Ireland, supported by the fledgling French revolutionary government. The French, again at war with Britain, came in too few numbers and too late to assist that rising too.

France's involvement in the 'British wars' ultimately done more harm than good for Scotland and Ireland, causing the Irish parliament to be abolished, and also contributing to the heavy garrisoning of the Scottish highlands and subsequent atrocities against civilians (most of which were committed by Scottish troops on fellow Scots.)

The bravery of the Scots and Irish exiles in the French service can never be doubted though, and with France's full support things could have been very different.

No British regiment has Culloden on its list of battle honours.

Glossary and order of battle

WAR OF THE AUSTRIAN SUCCESSION: Fought between 1740 and 1748, this conflict involved most of the major European powers, though it actually did little to change the balance of power on the continent. It all started because an Austrian princess was next in line to succeed to the powerful Hapsburg throne, and the pretext that a woman should not sit on that throne was used as an excuse to start the war.

France, Ireland's exiled army in French service, Prussia and Spain made up one side, the other side, known to posterity as ' The Pragmatic army' was made up of Britain, Hanover, Austria and the Dutch republic, among others. The war ended with the treaty of Aix-La-Chapelle in 1748.

MARSHALL MAURICE DE SAXE: Born one of eight illegitimate sons of King Augustus II of Poland in 1696, this shrewd military leader made his name in the French army in the first half of the eighteenth century and later became a naturalised Frenchman and Marshall of France. He was supposed to command the formidable French invasion force set to cross the channel to England in 1744 until bad weather ruined the enterprise. He was also a strong advocate of a substantial French landing in Essex in 1745 to support the Jacobites but, again, this plan came to nothing.

DUKE OF CUMBERLAND: The same age as his cousin Charles Edward, William Augustus Duke of Cumberland was the second and favourite son of King George II. He commanded the British army defeated by the French at Fontenoy in 1745, a French army that contained several regiments of the Irish brigade. Recalled to Britain to secure his father's throne and crush the Jacobite rising, he did so with vindictive earnestness earning himself the eternal nickname of 'butcher'. An average soldier, popular with his men, he drilled them at Aberdeen extensively prior to Culloden so that they could fire three times, rather than twice, a minute. This was to have devastating consequences for the clans who charged his lines on Drummossie moor, ensuring that they reached his lines in insufficient numbers to break them. He died in 1765, and interestingly was recently voted 'worst ever Briton' in a BBC poll.

PREST: French version of a method of fighting made famous by Scottish highlanders in the seventeenth and eighteenth centuries, the only real difference being that the French employed this tactic with bayonets. The French army learned to improve this method of fighting from the Irish brigade, who had become accustomed to fighting with edged weapons in the Williamite war of 1689-91, primarily because they had little else to fight with.

CUIMNIDH AR LUIMNEACH AGUS AR FEAL NE SASANACH: Gaelic battle cry of the Irish brigade in French service. In English, it means, "Remember Limerick and English betrayal"

BAYONET(S): Named after the Bayonne region of France where the weapon was first used as a hunting tool to 'finish off' animals that had been shot. The original Bayonet, known as the 'plug' bayonet, plugged into the muzzle of a musket and took time both to screw in and unplug. It also meant that the musket could not be fired while the bayonet was being fitted, leaving the musketeer vulnerable to hand to hand or cavalry attack. The plug bayonet was partly to blame for the Williamite line collapsing against the Jacobites at Killiecrankie in 1689. The Bayonet also heralded the demise of the pike in most European armies, as the weapon effectively turned each musketeer into a pikeman when necessary, though one man in five in most European armies still carried the weapon as a defence against cavalry until the first decade of the eighteenth century. The British army phased out it's last pikes in 1705, though the weapon was still used by irregular armies like that of the united Irishmen of 1798, chiefly because they couldn't get their hands on anything better. The plug Bayonet was later replaced by the socket bayonet, which fitted around the muzzle of the musket rather than down it, meaning the weapon could be fired with the bayonet fixed. Both sides used the socket bayonet in the 1745/46 rising by the time of Culloden. Variants of the socket Bayonet are still in use by armies today.

FLINTLOCK MUSKET: The flintlock musket first came into popular use in major Europeans wars in the late seventeenth century and replaced the older, unreliable matchlock system and the lesser used, expensive wheel lock system, both of which were used in the thirty years war and English civil war. It's principle advantages over the matchlock were that it used flint striking on metal as an ignition system rather than a burning matchchord like the matchlock, making the flintlock more reliable in adverse weather conditions, as well as making the soldier harder to see in the dark, something the glowing chord of a matchlock could give away.

The introduction of paper cartridges containing a ball and enough powder for a shot also made reloading the flintlock far easier and safer than fiddling with loose powder and shot like with the matchlock. The flintlock system proved the simplest and most durable design of infantry weapon from the 1680's up until well beyond the Napoleonic wars of the early nineteenth century. The weapon was accurate at no more than eighty yards and wildly inaccurate beyond that range, meaning it was best deployed en masse when fired in volleys. Good soldiers could fire three shots a minute. Cumberland's men trained vigorously at Aberdeen before Culloden until they could manage this feat, and the extra volley they could deliver after this training was to prove crucial.

MATCHLOCK MUSKET: A descendant of one of the first mass produced handguns, the arquebus, this weapon came to the fore in the sixteenth century but it was used mostly in the seventeenth century. It had to be fired in volleys due to it's inaccuracy and the vulnerability of musketeers while they reloaded had to be covered by blocks of men with pikes to stop them being ridden down by enemy cavalry. Unreliable in wet weather, it was probably last used in warfare in any great numbers by the outgunned Jacobites in the Williamite war of 1689-91 in Ireland. It was replaced both by the more reliable flintlock musket and the bayonet, thus combining pikeman and musketeer. A few matchlocks were used by the Jacobites at Prestonpans and on their march south through England, but by January 1746 every soldier in the Jacobite army had a French flintlock and bayonet, supplied by King Louis XV, or a carbine in the case of the cavalry. They often lacked sufficient ammunition with which to engage the Hanoverian regulars in a standard fire fight though.

BASKET HILTED BROADSWORD: Often mistakenly called a 'claymore' (the claymore was in fact a medieval two handed sword probably last swung in anger at Killiecrankie in 1689), this nevertheless fearsome weapon was carried by officers and financially better off men in the Jacobite army. Essentially a double edged blade with a basket metal hand grip, it was used at close quarters by the Clan's shock troops in the front line. It was later ironically adopted as a hand to hand weapon for highland troops in the British army and officers of highland regiments still carry them for ceremonial purposes today.

BRIGADIER STAPLETON: Brigadier Walter Stapleton was an exile in the French army who commanded part of the Jacobite second line, most of his duties focused on the small contingents of the Irish brigade and Royal Ecossaise. His rash comments at the council of war in Culloden house are partly, but by no means entirely, to blame for the Jacobites' ill fated decision to stand on Drummossie moor. His actual regiment was the Royal Ecossaise. He was mortally wounded at Culloden.

IRISH BRIGADE: Units of Irish exiles who fought in the service of France all over the world following the Williamite war. (1689-91)

They were originally five regiments of unarmed men 'swapped' by James II and VII with Louis XIV for a brigade of experienced French infantry to help with his ill fated Irish campaign of 1689-91, then their numbers were swelled by the twelve thousand men of James' Irish army repatriated to France following the treaty of Limerick.

Initially there were two Irish armies in French service, the Irish brigade and King James' own army in exile, though they were amalgamated into one army following the treaty of Ryswick in 1697 when Louis was forced to recognise William of Orange as the rightful king of Britain and disband James' army. The Irish brigade wore long skirted red coats as a symbol of their loyalty to the deposed house of Stuart, and because they considered themselves to be the legitimate British army, albeit in exile.

They served France until the revolution in 1789 when most of their officers returned home or sought service in other European armies.

DILLON'S: Named after their colonel, this was one of the first regiments sent to France as part of James II and Louis XIV's "deal". A small, red coated, detachment of them were present at Culloden, though they had earlier seen their ranks decimated by the siege of Stirling castle. They covered the rear in the final stages of Culloden and were treated as prisoners of war when they surrendered after running out of ammunition.

JAMES II AND VII: Rightful king of Britain who reigned from 1685 until he was deposed by a military coup in 1688. Prior to becoming King he was a brave soldier in the English regiments attached to the French army, though his experience was of commanding hundreds, rather than thousands, of men.

As he was a Roman Catholic, there were several attempts to have him excluded from succeeding his brother Charles II to the throne, but when he ascended the throne he still inherited a massively royalist parliament and widespread popular support. An attempt to replace him on the throne with an illegitimate Protestant son of Charles II named James, Duke of Monmouth, was easily crushed by James' powerful standing army at Sedgemoor in 1685, largely thanks to the military abilities of James' best friend and most able soldier, John Churchill, an ancestor of Winston Churchill, later the Duke of Marlborough. James' interference with the church of England and his powerful, increasingly Catholic standing army were gradually treated with more and more suspicion as his reign wore on, though his subjects tolerated him as he was in his fifties and the throne was due to pass to his protestant daughter Mary, who had married William of Orange, Dutch Stadholder and leader of a pan European alliance against James' ally, the militantly Catholic and expansionist, Louis XIV.

Things changed when James had a son by his second wife Mary of Modena in 1688 and the child was duly baptized a Catholic. Fearing a Catholic dynasty, seven treacherous English statesmen invited William of Orange to invade and 'restore English liberties', which he did.

James' powerful army, despite a few hundred defections to William, could easily have destroyed William but James, who had already seen one civil war tear England apart and was perhaps haunted by the ghost of his beheaded father Charles I, dithered. At this crucial time he was betrayed by his best friend and most able soldier, Colonel Churchill, who defected to William after being tipped off that he was to be arrested on suspicion of treason. When James' other daughter Anne also defected to William, James, betrayed by his best friend and his family, chose to disband his army and spare his country yet another civil war, fleeing to France and the protection of Louis XIV. There were minor skirmishes between James' loyal troops and William's invaders at Reading and Wincanton, though the largely bloodless nature of this coup has led it to be known as 'the glorious revolution'.

With Louis's backing James landed in 1689 in overwhelmingly Catholic Ireland, and with his French troops set about securing the country and raising an army with which to regain his throne. Resistance in Ulster slowed his progress though, giving William time to put together a counter invasion. James' army was poorly equipped, poorly trained and poorly supplied while William's army were experienced, well armed European mercenaries, William wisely not taking the British army to Ireland as he (correctly) feared they would not fight against their former King.

James' Irish campaign failed after the inconclusive battle of the Boyne and the bloodbath at Aughrim a year later, his troops surrendering under very favourable terms in 1691 having fought the Williamites to a standstill. Most of his army was to rejoin him in France. Myths of James' cowardice and about the reason for his returning to France after the Boyne have since been proved to be Williamite propaganda and utter lies.

A rising in Scotland in 1689 by James' supporters also came to nothing, despite initial success over the Williamites at the battle of Killiecrankie. William punished this rising by ordering the infamous Glencoe massacre of 1692.

James lived in the palace of St Germain in France for the rest of his days, and though there were numerous plots to restore him in England they all came to nothing. His ally Louis was forced to recognise William as king of Britain in 1697 meaning James' army in exile was disbanded and he received no further aid from Louis, though Louis still gave his old friend a generous pension. James died of a brain haemorrhage in 1701, his claim to the throne now passing to his son, also called James, the baby who had caused all the trouble in 1688. He was known to his supporters as James III and VIII, and to his enemies as 'the old pretender'.

TREATY OF LIMERICK: 1691 treaty that ended the Williamite war in Ireland and saw the transportation of James II's army to France in what became known as "the flight of the wild geese". James' supporters had continued the war in his absence and fought the Williamites to a standstill but were besieged by the Williamites, now Commanded by Danish General Ginkell.

The treaty had two articles, one of these articles was military, where members of James' Jacobite army were given the option of either sailing to France to join James in exile, or of joining the Williamite army, most choosing the former.

The second article dealt with civil matters, whereby the Catholic Irish were promised religious toleration and that Catholic landowners would not be dispossessed. Ginkel also promised, in good faith, that there would be no reprisals against the Catholics or those who had supported James. Among others, the treaty was signed by Patrick Sarsfield for the Jacobites/Irish and Ginkell for the Williamites. Sarsfield and his French advisors saw no alternative before signing and believed they had got the best deal possible for Ireland. Even when a French fleet arrived with substantial reinforcements and supplies after he had signed, Sarsfield refused to break his word of honour and carry on the war, opting to join his men and his King in France. Ginkell too remained true to his word, but the treaty he had brokered was torn up and broken by the English parliament as soon as the Irish army had departed, and a series of harsh reprisals and penal laws were imposed upon the Irish Catholics in the years that followed, those who had supported James now being without their army and completely defenceless.

JACOBUS: Latin for James, giving itself to the term 'Jacobite' meaning supporters of James, who unsuccessfully tried to restore the direct Stuart line to the throne of Great Britain in 1689-91, 1708, 1715, 1719, 1745/56 and 1759.

WILLIAM OF ORANGE: Leader of the Dutch republic and figurehead of the league of Augsburg, a pan European alliance against Louis XIV's Catholic France and it's aggressive expansion policies. His official title was 'Stadtholder' in Holland.

In Britain he is seen as a symbol of resolute Protestantism, but the league of Augsburg which he so effectively organised was made up of both Catholic and Protestant nations, and was fully supported by the Catholic church and the Pope himself.

He married James II's Protestant daughter Mary, who was next in line to the British thrones until the unexpected birth of James' Catholic son in 1688. Seeing that Britain's dynasty would now be Catholic and knowing that there would be British troops involved in his war with Louis XIV, he accepted an invitation to invade England and oust James so as to ensure that any British troops in the war would be on his side. It was his desire to manipulate English foreign policy that made him take the gamble on invading England and deposing his own father in law, rather than any desire to rule Britain. His concern was always, first and foremost, the security of the Dutch republic and the battle against Louis XIV. He is seen as a hero by some Northern Ireland protestants as his success in the Williamite war began a protestant ascendancy in Ireland, though he himself had little love for the Ulstermen in his army, using them as cannon fodder, and he himself remained in Ireland for only a fortnight.

His marriage to Mary was political and they had no children, unsurprising given William's latent homosexuality. His military abilities were average, but his excellent diplomatic skills held together the league of Augsburg and its mix of Catholic and Protestant armies.

A popular painting and mural of William shows him crossing the Boyne on a white horse, but in actual fact that image is from a painting of William depicting the siege of Namur in modern Belgium. William was mounted on a black charger at the Boyne, according to all reliable sources.

There were several English plots to overthrow the increasingly unpopular William (Mary died in 1694) and replace him with James in the mid 1690's, chiefly instigated by James' daughter Anne and the duplicitous turncoat Churchill, though a spell in the tower of London soon convinced the latter to remain loyal to William. James' attempts to invade England with a French army saw Anne once again break off contact with her father.

William died of pneumonia in 1702 and was succeeded by Anne, the last Stuart monarch, who reigned until dying childless in 1714. The British throne then passed to the house of Hanover.

FLIGHT OF THE WILD GEESE: Term applied to the transfer of James II and VII's army to France from Ireland under the terms of the treaty of Limerick which ended the Williamite war there. "Wild geese" was the French codeword for troops smuggled from Ireland to France thereafter, and that's what the troops were listed as in ship's logs. The British government made joining foreign armies illegal in 1745 meaning that many Irish troops risked their lives by trying to reach France, though around the same time it's worth noting that recruitment of Irish troops into the British army soared (reaching a peak of one in three men by the time of the Napoleonic wars), which suggests that not all of the 'Wild geese' were exiles, many joined up for economic reasons. The term 'wild geese' is also used generally to describe Irish troops who have fought in countless foreign wars.

WILLIAMITE: Supporters of William of Orange's usurping of the British crowns in 1688/89, though the term chiefly refers to William's supporters and troops in his campaigns in Scotland and Ireland of 1689-91.

HANOVERIAN: Supporters of the house of Hanover, the German protestant dynasty who were given the British throne in 1714 in a bit to block the accession of the rightful claimant, James Francis Edward Stuart or 'the old pretender'. Dozens of other claimants were passed over in favour of the house of Hanover as they were safely and wholly Protestant. In a military context the term applies to those who were in arms against the Jacobites in 1715, 1719 and 1745/46.

CHARLES EDWARD STUART: Son of the old pretender and often referred to as 'the young pretender', but he is generally known to posterity as Bonnie Prince Charlie. Landed in Scotland in 1745 and raised a highland army in an attempt to regain his father's rightful throne. His only previous military experience was as a spectator at a siege in Italy as a teenager. His personality and Stuart blood were instrumental in getting some clans to 'come out' in his support, often against their better judgement as most of the arms and all of the men he brought with him from France failed to arrive. He only commanded in battle once, at Culloden, where he was of course utterly defeated. In the wider European context of things he was a pawn, used by the French in attempts to de-stabilise Britain, and he was the figurehead of two huge French invasion plans of 1744 and 1759, both of which came to nothing thanks to bad weather and the Royal Navy. He evaded capture after Culloden despite a £30,000 price tag on his head, and made it back to France where he was initially treated as a hero. A Roman Catholic, he later converted to Anglicanism in a forlorn attempt to make himself more appealing to would be supporters in Britain after 1746, but this done him no good. He died in Rome a dissolute drunk in 1788 and with him died the direct Stuart male line as his brother Henry became a cardinal and therefore had no children. Charles did have some illegitimate offspring though, and various crackpots around the world claim to be descended from him.

HOUSE OF HANOVER: European Protestant dynasty hailing from Germany who were promised the English crown by the 1701 act of settlement in the event of Queen Anne dying childless, which she did in 1714. The crown was originally promised to Electress Sophia of Hanover but by the time Queen Anne died this clam had passed to her son George, who became George I of Great Britain.

ROYAL ECCOSAISSE: Regiment of Jacobite Scottish exiles raised in France by the exiled Drummond family in 1744, originally intended to be part of the ill fated 1744 Franco Jacobite invasion attempt. The regiment was sent to Scotland late in 1745 to aid the rebellion and a second battalion was raised in Scotland. They wore blue coats with white diagonal cross belts to symbolise the cross of St Andrew and were properly equipped regular troops. Along with the three companies of the Irish brigade they provided the Jacobite army's firepower, though both units lost a lot of men during the pointless siege of Stirling castle. The second battalion contained some deserters from the Hanoverian army and was less well dressed and equipped than the first. Along with the Irish troops they covered the rear during the final stages of Culloden and were allowed to surrender honourably, the vast majority of them, unlike most of the other Jacobite prisoners, being treated as prisoners of war and exchanged later. They lost more than half their number at Culloden. Literally translated the regiment's name means 'Royal Scots' and they briefly exchanged volleys with the Hanoverian Royal Scots regiment towards the end of the battle.

FITZ-JAMES' HORSE: Heavy cavalry regiment of Scots and Irish exiles named after their founder, the Duke of Berwick, though the unit has went under some other names. They wore red coats and tricorn hats, not unlike their Hanoverian mounted counterparts. The whole regiment was sent to Scotland late in 1745, but three of the four squadrons and all of the regiment's horses were captured en route by the Royal Navy. By the time of Culloden the men of Fitz-James' had been mounted at the expense of Kilmarnock's horse and along with the Prince's blue coated life guards they bore the heavy burden of providing the Jacobite army's reconnaissance, communications and cavalry duties.

They were instrumental along with two lowland regiments in keeping the Ruthven road open allowing the routed Jacobite right and centre to escape before they surrendered and were treated as prisoners of war, save for the small contingent of about twelve men who helped escort the Prince from the battlefield.

BATTLE OF FALKIRK: Fought on January 17th 1746. Eight thousand government troops under General Hawley attempting to break the siege of Stirling castle were met by about seven thousand Jacobites, under Lord George Murray, just outside Falkirk. Hawley's attempt to scatter the highlanders with his cavalry backfired when the clans delivered two well disciplined volleys at point blank range, decimating the charge and sending the rest of the Hanoverian horsemen fleeing backwards riding through and scattering some of their own infantry. The Jacobites then seized the initiative and attacked, easily driving off infantry in the government centre and left. Ominously for the Jacobites though the government right held it's ground against the highland onslaught, and was only driven from the field by the timely intervention of the newly arrived Franco-Irish regular units and their disciplined musket volleys. The biggest battle of the '45, it ultimately achieved very little for the Jacobites as they couldn't pursue the defeated government army. Neither side deployed any artillery in this battle, the Hanoverians because of poor weather, the Jacobites because all their guns were otherwise employed bombarding Stirling castle.

Government losses were three hundred and fifty killed and another three hundred captured. The Jacobites lost some fifty men killed and another seventy wounded.

ARGYLE MILITIA: Pro government clans raised mostly from Clan Campbell. Armed with British muskets as well as more traditional weapons, they were responsible for a lot of the atrocities after Culloden that have since been blamed on the regular army. Used mostly as skirmishers and light infantry by the Hanoverian army.

CLAN CAMPBELL: Men chiefly from Argyle who, since the glorious revolution and the union of 1707, were notoriously anti Jacobite. See also Argyle militia (above).

CANNONGATE: Part of the lower end of the Royal mile that goes from Edinburgh castle to the palace of Holyrood. Traditionally home of the city's tollbooth and many taverns, now a modern street which thrives on tourism.

JACOBITE RISINGS OF 1715 AND 1719:
Two attempts to restore the Stuarts, both of which ended in failure.

1715: The Jacobites under the earl of Mar raised some ten thousand men and this rising was typified by it's slogan of "King James and no union". It enjoyed widespread public support thanks to disaffection with the union and the unpopularity of Britain's new King George I, who couldn't even speak English. The rising coincided with a Jacobite rising in

127

northern England led by the Earl of Derenwater, who received some reinforcements from the Scottish Jacobites. The Scots Jacobites were fought to a standstill but not defeated by government troops under the Duke of Argyle at the indecisive battle of Sherrifmuir, after which the rising lost momentum, despite the belated arrival of King James at Peterhead. The army melted away, though there were few reprisals by the Hanoverians. The English Jacobites were surrounded and compelled to surrender at Preston, Derenwater later being executed and many of his troops being transported to the Americas as slaves.

1719: Cardinal Alberoni and Spain sent two expeditions to Britain in an attempt restore the Stuarts. The main fleet and force of five thousand men was scattered by a storm but two ships containing arms, money and three hundred Spanish regulars did make it to Scotland and were joined by a few clans, including a certain Rob Roy McGregor. Arguments between the Jacobite leadership delayed and hampered mobilisation though, allowing government troops under General Whightman to intercept and defeat them in a small engagement at Glensheil. Again, the clans melted away and the Spanish regulars surrendered honourably as prisoners of war.

KILLIECRANKIE: Battle fought on July 27th 1689 between just over two thousand Jacobite highlanders, mostly infantry, led by John Graham of Claverhouse or "bonnie Dundee", and Williamite forces under General Hugh Mackay numbering around three and a half thousand men. After the two armies stared at each other taking desultory pot shots for most of the day, Dundee's army advanced at around seven pm so that the Williamite troops had the sun in their eyes. The Highlanders fired what few firearms they had and charged headlong at the Williamite lines, receiving two thunderous volleys from MacKay's men, which killed or wounded around a third of the Jacobites. MacKay's troops were, however, equipped with plug bayonets and most his men didn't have time to screw them into their muskets before the clansmen were upon them with cold steel. The result was a bloodbath, MacKay's army losing some two thousand men killed and the rest being put to flight. Though a resounding Jacobite victory, Dundee was killed in the battle and his army lost heart to a degree. They were later checked at the battle of Dunkeld and then routed at Cromdale the following year, ending James II and VII's hopes in Scotland, for the time being at least. These events led to the infamous Glencoe massacre of 1692.

PATRICK SARSFIELD: Legendary Irish hero and Jacobite who made his name in the Williamite war of 1689-91. A born leader and superb cavalryman he fought in the English regiments of Charles II attached to the French army until being recalled to England in 1685 upon the ascension to the throne of James II. James gave him a colonelcy for his part in suppressing the Monmouth rebellion of 1685.

Sarsfield and his men fired the only shots of the 'glorious revolution' when they skirmished with Williamite troops at Wincanton and Reading. He later joined the exiled James in France and then accompanied him to Ireland and was instrumental in helping raise an Irish army to supplement the French brigade loaned to James by Louis XIV. He fought with distinction at the inconclusive battle of the Boyne in 1690 and later captured a vast amount of Williamite stores and ammunition in a daring raid, which bogged down the Williamites for a further year. He fought in the bloodbath of Aughrim in 1691 and twice successfully defended Limerick from the Williamites. When James' cause in Ireland was clearly failing he helped end the war by negotiating the very favourable treaty of Limerick, which the English later reneged on. After this he was made a General in the French army and fought with distinction in Flanders before being mortally wounded at the battle of Landen in 1693. His last words were **"If this was only for Ireland"**.

BATTLE OF THE BOYNE: Fought on July 1ˢᵗ 1690 between the Franco-Irish Jacobite army of King James and the forces of the league of Augsburg, led by William of Orange. This was the last time two men who had been crowned king of England faced each other on the battlefield, though the war itself was more to do with the continental struggle between William and France's Louis XIV.

William's army was made up of Protestants and Catholics and was superbly armed, equipped and supplied, numbering some thirty six thousand men, most of whom were Dutch, German, Danish, Scandinavian and Swiss, supplemented by a few Ulstermen and Scots. They had the full support of the Pope and William's Catholic Dutch blue guards carried the papal banner into this battle. All of William's men carried modern flintlock muskets and had plenty of ammunition.

In contrast, James' army, led by French General, the Comte de Lazuan, numbered just twenty five thousand men. James had some five thousand French regular infantry and a thousand French Cavalry, as well as two thousand crack Irish horsemen, who were to prove his best troops as they were made up of the Catholic gentry who had been dispossessed and consequently had great interest in seeing James restored.

The rest of James' army however, save for one or two good infantry regiments, were poorly trained, ill equipped peasant conscripts. Those who were lucky enough to have muskets had obsolete matchlock weapons sent from France and of general poor quality, Louis XIV later admitting that he had sent the Irish 'the sweepings from his armouries'. There was also a serious shortage of gunpowder and shot in James' army. Most of his Irish conscripts were armed with pikes, swords, farm tools, rocks and even their bare hands. They were however, highly motivated as they were defending their faith. On paper James' army had no chance. He was not helped by the fact that his general Lazuan had secret orders from Louis XIV not to use the French units if at all possible.

The two armies faced each other outside Drogheda on opposite sides of the Boyne. William sent ten thousand men on a march west to outflank James and James took the bait, sending most of his army, including the French infantry and most of his cannon, west to meet them. However they were not able to engage each other thanks to a boggy ravine, and the two forces sat all afternoon staring at each other.

William then unleashed his true attack across the river Boyne, where James' five thousand infantry and three thousand cavalry now faced twenty six thousand of William's men. Outgunned and outnumbered, James' infantry at the crossing were pushed back and it was left to the Jacobite cavalry to hold the Boyne, which they did heroically for several hours until sheer weight of numbers and their own heavy casualties forced them to conduct a successful fighting retreat. In reality this was no great Williamite victory, though it did force the Jacobites to abandon Dublin and retreat west to hold the line of the Shannon. Casualties usually given are five hundred Williamites killed to fifteen hundred Jacobites killed, but included in the Jacobite 'casualties' are seven hundred and fifty men of James' French brigade who were actually German prisoners of war conscripted into French service who defected to William when Dublin fell. If anything, it's remarkable that James' army lasted as long as it did that day. In his memoirs James claimed the Boyne as a successful rearguard action, and there is a lot of truth in that claim, though he was still ultimately forced to retreat.

AUGHRIM: The bloodiest battle in Irish history, this was the battle that really began the end of the Williamite war in Ireland. Fought on July 12th 1691 in county Galway between the Franco-Irish Jacobites now led by French General St Ruth and Patrick Sarsfield, and the Williamite army now commanded by Danish general Ginkell.

The Jacobites had about eighteen thousand men, the Williamites had twenty thousand.

King James and William of Orange had both long since departed Ireland.

St Ruth had picked an excellent defensive position with a series of trenches and a castle holding one flank. A Williamite assault on his exposed other flank was easily repulsed then a bloodbath ensued as the Williamites launched a frontal attack in the centre. Again, the Jacobites repulsed this and Sarsfield counter attacked with the cavalry, spiking a battery of Williamite guns. It looked like a Jacobite victory was imminent, until St Ruth was decapitated by a cannonball.

A third Williamite assault on the other Jacobite flank proved successful as the castle's Irish defenders had been issued with British ammunition that didn't fit into their French supplied muskets. Jacobite cavalry posted there to cover that eventuality were ordered to withdraw by their commander Henry Lutrell rather than counter attack as ordered and eventually the Williamites won the day. Lutrell later proved to be a Williamite spy and was assassinated in Dublin later. Aughrim was utter carnage. Three thousand Williamites and four thousand Jacobites were killed outright, and another four thousand Jacobite soldiers ran away, but what was disastrous for the Jacobites was the loss of the vast majority of their officers and their much loved French General. This was the last major pitched battle of the Williamite war.

PRESS GANG: Groups of individuals whose task it was to force (impress) men into the service of the King, an at the time legal practice. Predominantly used to fill the ranks of the navy, but often used by the army to swell it's ranks from time to time. Victims would usually be plied with alcohol then carted off to the nearest recruitment depot or, if the need for men was more urgent, literally beaten unconscious then carried off.

FRANCO JACOBITE INVASION OF 1744: One of the few occasions when the French seemed genuinely keen to substantially aid the exiled Stuarts in their quest to regain the throne, largely thanks to their being many senior French generals and politicians with Jacobite sympathies in favour at Versailles at the time. A substantial invasion force, with Charles Edward Stuart as it's figure head and commanded by Marshal Saxe, consisting of thousands of battle hardened French regulars alongside the entire Irish brigade, a battle fleet and troop transports, was set to invade England from Dunkirk. The plan was abandoned when much of the fleet was wrecked by a storm and many of the soldiers drowned, much to the frustration of Charles and the French. It deterred Charles little though, and he set out alone the next year in a mere two ships with eight hundred men of the Irish brigade, destined for Scotland.

KINGSTON'S HORSE: Regiment of volunteer cavalry raised in Nottinghamshire and named after their de facto colonel, the Duke of Kingston. Raised specifically to crush the '45, they were disbanded soon afterwards. Since they were newly raised and the troopers weren't regulars they behaved in a most beastly manner, especially in the pursuit after Culloden when they cut down many innocent civilians including women and children along the Inverness road.

FURLOUGH: Authorised temporary leave of absence from the army. Many of the men in Fitz James' horse and the Irish brigade at Culloden were in Scotland on extended furlough, having volunteered to fight for the Prince.

BATTLE OF PRESTONPANS: First major engagement of the '45 fought just outside Edinburgh on September 21st 1745. Both sides were more or less evenly matched numerically at around 2300 men each but the Hanoverians, on paper at least, under sir John Cope, had the advantage as they had cavalry and artillery, whilst the Jacobites only had about fifty horsemen who acted as the Prince's lifeguard.

Cope took up a strong position with a ditch to his front and walled enclosures protecting his right flank, but he was outsmarted when a local Jacobite sympathiser named John Anderson offered to lead the clansmen along a secret path through a thought to be impassable marsh so that when morning came the Jacobites had appeared in the opposite direction from where Cope had expected them.

The clans charged out of the early morning mist, many bearing ancient weapons as no modern arms had yet arrived from France, completely surprising and routing the government army. The ditch and walls Cope thought would protect his men now acted as barriers to their escape. The government troops managed one ragged volley before running away, and this inept fusillade cost the Jacobites a mere thirty men killed and a further seventy men wounded. The government losses were astronomical, three hundred men killed, five hundred wounded and around fifteen hundred taken prisoner, almost the entire army. Only Cope himself with some of his officers and cavalry escaped. The Jacobites treated the wounded and captured Hanoverian troops decently and humanely, offering food, shelter and medical care. This is in stark contrast to how the Jacobites were treated after Culloden.

COUNCIL OF WAR IN DERBY: Meeting that took place in Exeter house between the fourth and sixth of December 1745 between the Jacobite high command. Despite having made remarkable progress through England with virtually no opposition, the Jacobite army had received barely three hundred recruits along the way, and two Hanoverian armies were closing in on them, both of these armies being bigger than the Prince's. The Prince and his Franco Irish advisors had wanted to press on to London, only one hundred and twenty miles away, but the Clan chiefs were all for returning to Scotland to consolidate and obtain more recruits, as well as suppressing the Clans loyal to the government who had taken up arms as soon as they had left Scotland. A few French regulars and some much needed arms and ammunition had also arrived in Scotland from France making the argument even stronger for returning home. In the end, the debate was swayed by the timely intervention of a government spy claiming to be a Jacobite sympathiser who brought false news of a third, fictitious government army of ten thousand men blocking their path to the capital. To the chiefs this was the final straw. Charles had won the vote to invade England by a single vote, this time he lost by a substantial majority. His relationship with the Highlanders was never quite the same after this and he henceforth continued to rely more on his Franco Irish officers for advice. The retreat began on December 6th. If only the Jacobites had known that the French had belatedly put together a strong invasion force ready to cross the channel in their support should they march on London, and that London was virtually undefended save for a hastily assembled ragtag militia. Londoners were always fans of the winning side and had the Jacobites scattered London's pitiful defenders and seized the exchequer and parliament there is every chance that a similar situation to that of 1688 would have led to Charles's father being restored, if he accepted certain conditions. Whether or not England would have accepted a Catholic king who arrived with an army supplied by Britain's enemy is another matter, but it worked in 1688 so could feasibly have been successful in 1745 too. Alas we will never know, as the Jacobite's road didn't lead south now, it lead north, and ultimately to Culloden. With the information the Jacobites had at the time it WAS the logical decision to retreat and consolidate, but it was also the WRONG one.

DUDLEY BRADSTREET: Hanoverian spy who conveniently turned up at the Jacobites' council of war in Derby, seemingly presenting impeccable Jacobite credentials, and who brought false news of a fictitious Hanoverian army between Charles's men and London. The Jacobites were probably going to retreat anyway but Bradstreet was the 'straw that broke the camel's back' in that respect.

MACPHERSON OF CLUNY'S: Elite clan unit of about four hundred men who joined the Jacobite army in 1745. They played a vital role in Lord George Murray's rearguard action against Cumberland's advance guard at Clifton, but were absent from Culloden as they had been sent on another mission. Charles was strongly advised to await their return before fighting at Culloden. They did make it back to Ruthven but were disbanded when the Prince dispersed his army and returned home to France.

CLIFTON: Hotly pursued by Cumberland and some four thousand cavalry and mounted infantry, Lord George Murray and some of the best highland units in the Jacobite army made a stand on Clifton moor in Cumbria, to allow the rest of the army a chance of escape. In total around one thousand dismounted Hanoverian dragoons faced Murray and the regiments of McPherson of Cluny, Stewarts of Appin, Macdonalds of Glengarry and John Roy Stewart's Edinburgh regiment. Contrary to the popular stereotype of the highlander charging sword and shield in hand, this was a standard musket fire fight in which the clans proved themselves to be just as effective with their muskets as they were with cold steel, inflicting a serious bloody nose on the pursuing Hanoverians with their disciplined musketry before finally chasing them off. This quite brilliant rearguard action allowed the main Jacobite army to continue it's retreat north unmolested. It was pretty one sided too, one hundred of Cumberland's men killed for only twelve Jacobite casualties.

SIEGE OF STIRLING CASTLE: On the Jacobites' return to Scotland their numbers were swelled by the arrival of around a thousand Franco-Irish regulars and more highland and lowland volunteers, bringing their numbers to around eight thousand men.

They then decided to besiege Stirling castle, despite lacking sufficient heavy artillery to do so effectively. This also made Charles's men very unpopular with the inhabitants of Stirling itself as counter fire from the castle caused considerable damage to the town, a deliberate tactic of the castle's Hanoverian garrison who were expecting to be relieved. The highland troops simply weren't interested in siege work and consequently most of the siege was conducted by the newly arrived regulars of the Royal Ecossaise and Irish brigade. These units suffered heavy casualties in the siege from sniping, counter bombardment, exposure and sallies from the garrison, casualties that the Jacobites could ill afford in such well equipped experienced units. These crack troops were wasted by this rather pointless siege.

HIGHLAND CHARGE: A romantic title applied to the sometimes unconventional way that highland units fought in the seventeenth and eighteenth centuries. The usually accepted version of 'the charge' is that the clans would advance to within musket range of their opponents, discharge whatever firearms they had in a single volley, and then rush in headlong with sword, shield, axe or bayonet, spreading terror and panic in their opponents. In truth this was not an actual battle tactic but more of a necessity as the highland troops usually lacked sufficient ammunition to engage their opponents in a standard fire fight, so cold steel and rushing in was a necessity of combat rather than a pre defined tactic. This is evident in what was left behind on Drummossie Moor after the battle, over a thousand French muskets with bayonets and less than two hundred broadswords. All major European armies at the time employed this tactic, but conventional forces usually indulged in protracted exchanges of musket fire before rushing in with bayonet or sword. The French version of the 'highland charge' for example, was called a 'prest' attack. The clans fought like that because they HAD to, not because it was 'their way of fighting'.

LE PRINCE CHARLES: Ship full of French gold bound for the Jacobite army that was lost early in 1746. The loss of this gold meant that the Jacobite army had to be paid in meal rather than in money, meaning that when their last remaining meal store in Inverness was threatened, they were obliged to fight at Culloden to defend it.

KING GEORGE II: Second Hanoverian monarch to sit on the throne of Britain and far more popular than his father George I, not only because he spoke English, something his father never bothered to learn, but because he was the last king of Britain to serve on the battlefield, at Dettingen in 1743. He reigned from 1727 until 1760.

CAMERON OF LOCHEIL: Chief of Clan Cameron, whose eight hundred men provided the backbone of the Jacobite army when it was first raised in the autumn of 1745. He had put together a coherent realistic plan to put some twenty thousand highland troops into the field in 1744 should the planned Franco Jacobite invasion take place and if the French sent a few battalions of regulars to Scotland to guard the highlanders as they mobilised. Of course, neither plan came to fruition and the Camerons came out on their own for the '45. Known to posterity as 'the gentle Lochiel' primarily as he had ensured that Hanoverian prisoners and wounded were cared for humanely and because he had prevented highland troops from sacking both Glasgow and Edinburgh.

Bitterly opposed to invading England after Prestonpans and an advocate of retreat while the army dithered at Derby, he was wounded at the battle of Falkirk and then sent with a detachment of the army to besiege the government garrison of Fort William until recalled to Culloden in April 1746, just in time for the battle. His clan regiment lost more than half its number killed charging the government muskets at Culloden and he himself had his ankles shattered by grape shot. He later escaped to rejoin his Prince in France and to implore the French to send more arms men and gold to Scotland to aid the small scale guerrilla style campaign that had continued in the Prince's absence under Lochiel's brother. Given command of a French regiment in 1747 he was killed the following year fighting in Flanders.

EPISCOPALIAN: Christian denomination with it's own distinct identity from the seventeenth century onwards. They retained bishops and much of the ceremony of the old Catholic church while still being Protestant.

PRESBYTERIAN: Scotland's national form of Christianity derived from a form of Calvinism that was made Scotland's national faith in 1560, chiefly because it's biggest champion, John Knox, wanted to marry the sixteen year old daughter of a prominent landowner who stood to benefit greatly from the proposed redistribution of church lands. It differed from the Episcopalian church in that it was run by a general assembly rather than by bishops, and was much more of a 'no frills' faith with little ceremony.

VERSAILLE: Seat of French government from 1682 until the revolution in 1789. France's wars were directed from this location and it's impressive palace. Louis XIV and Louis XV received and directed all Jacobite related dispatches from Versaille.

NCO: Non commissioned officer, like a Corporal or Sergeant, usually an enlisted man who had seniority over his peers or had distinguished himself in some way.

SUBALTERN: Officer of junior rank below that of Captain, usually a Lieutenant first or second.

SQUADRON: Term usually applied to a body of cavalry numbering anything from sixty to one hundred and twenty men.

COMMISIONED OFFICER: Soldier usually of the rank of Lieutenant or above, who is commissioned by his government to lead soldiers and follow the orders of his superiors and hold a position of command and responsibility. Generally better treated and paid than enlisted men, an officer can resign his commission at any time and leave the army, unlike enlisted men and NCO's.

PUNIC WARS: Series of wars fought between 264BC and 146BC, the protagonists being the North African city state of Carthage and the fledgling Roman empire. Despite great successes under Hannibal, Carthage was ultimately defeated and razed to the ground. The wars are famous for the simplistic tactics used by both sides due to the limitation of weaponry, and for their extreme brutality.

THE PRETENDER: Derived from the nicknames given to Charles Edward Stuart and his father by their political opponents, Charles was often referred to simply as 'the pretender' by his enemies while he was on British soil. They were called 'the young pretender' and 'the old pretender' respectively as they still held what they considered to be legitimate British courts in exile and were still able to raise taxes from loyal supporters in Britain.

KINGS EVIDENCE: A way by which convicted men or traitors could have their sentence reduced or even admonished providing that they changed sides or turned informer on those who had helped them. We would now refer to such a person as a 'supergrass'.

STEWARTS OF APPIN: Staunchly Jacobite clan whose men had the honour of being first to break the government line at Culloden. They suffered heavily in the ultimately futile attack though. The half brother of the Clan's chief was hanged in 1752 for the murder of Colin Campbell who had replaced the dispossessed Alan Breck Stewart when the Stewart lands were forfeited as punishment for their role in the risings. This murder was immortalised in the novel 'kidnapped' by Robert Louis Stevenson.

ERIN GO BRAGH: Anglicised Irish Gaelic version of a phrase literally meaning 'Ireland forever'.

CALIBRE: The Diameter of the inside of a gun barrel, the term is also used to categorise ammunition size.

CARBINE: Smaller, lighter version of the musket, used by cavalry as it was easier to handle from the saddle. The carbine is also a general term for the lighter muskets or rifles carried by horsemen throughout the centuries though it is now used to describe simple shorted versions of infantry longarms, a prime example of this being the M1 Garrand carbine used by American officers during world war two.

MUZZLE: The open end of a firearm barrel from which the bullet/projectile is fired. Most infantry firearms were muzzle loaded until the invention of the percussion system in nineteenth century America in the case of handguns, or the breech loading rifle like the Prussian needle gun or British Martini Henry in the late 1860's. Muzzle loaders were much slower to load than breech loaders.

BRITISH SQUARES: The hollow square was an infantry tactic that first appeared in Europe in the late seventeenth century as a counter measure to cavalry following the rise of the combined musketeer/bayonet man and the decline of the pike. Despite what you may see in films, horses will not charge onto hedges of Bayonets arrayed in such a way, though human beings were often stupid enough to be induced to do so. Infantry deployed in squares caused enemy cavalry to mill around them uselessly while volleys of musket fire from the squares downed the horsemen. A highly effective tactic, it was abandoned by most European armies in the mid eighteenth century as advances in firearms had made cavalry charges against mass infantry formations near suicidal. It was re adopted later in Britain and France's colonial wars in Africa and India/Asia as, although they often had much superior firepower, they often faced ludicrously enormous enemy forces who surrounded them. The square was probably last used by the French foreign legion in Africa or by the British in the Sudan in the 1880's.

TARGE: Round shield often studded with metal and made from layers of wood and leather, carried by many highland troops. Effective at parrying bayonet and sword thrusts. Ballistic testing has disproved the romantic myth that this weapon could stop a musket ball at effective range. I myself have seen a brown bess fired at about eighty yards at a 'targe' and not only did it go through the shield and imbed itself a full inch into a block of ballistic soap, it also filled the ballistic soap (which represented the soldier carrying the targe) with a multitude of wooden splinters, showing the horrific wounds that a highlander's shield could inflict on him if he use it to hide from musket fire. The targe was undoubtedly a useful hand to hand weapon though.

DIRK: Small, but by no means minute, dagger often carried by front line highland shock troops in the same hand they carried their targe. It was a secondary weapon though, and only the best swordsmen could combine it with targe and basket hilted broadsword.

FRANCO-IRISH OFFICERS: Irish exiles who usually joined France's Irish Brigade. In the '45 the Prince's two main Franco Irish advisors were John Sheridan and Colonel John William O'Sullivan. History has been very unkind to these two men and they are often blamed for the rising failing and particularly for the defeat at Culloden. In reality both were experienced soldiers and must have been exasperated at having so few regular troops to command and such an amateurish set up to contend with, a far cry from the well oiled war machine that was the French regular army or indeed the Irish brigade itself.

ADC: Aide de camp, personal assistant to a middle or high ranking officer.

ELCHO: Lord Elcho, the Prince's ADC and commander of his blue coated mounted Life guards. Fought bravely in all the engagements of the '45 and later escaped to France where he joined the French army and spent time as a captain in Fitz-James' horse and as Colonel of the Royal Ecossaise, two regiments who were also at Culloden. He is often credited with having shouted the immortal phrase 'run you cowardly Italian' at Prince Charles but it's worth noting that Elcho himself escaped too. He died peacefully in Paris in 1787.

LORD GEORGE MURRAY: By far the most able commander of highland troops in the Jacobite army and with a keen eye for suitable ground, it was a surprise when Murray joined the Jacobites in 1745 as he had taken part in the earlier risings of 1715 and 1719, for which he had received a royal pardon in 1724. An experienced soldier, Murray deserves credit for the victories at Prestonpans and Falkirk, and for his quite brilliant rearguard action at Clifton during the retreat from Derby. He protested bitterly about the choice of battlefield at Culloden, where he was relieved of command of the whole army and given only the right wing, the right wing unsurprisingly being the most effective in the doomed attack. He also protested bitterly at the Prince's decision to disband what was left of his army when it re assembled at Ruthven after the battle, believing that a guerrilla style campaign was highly plausible. One of the more flawed sides to Murray's character was that he was stubborn and would listen to advice from no one.

Murray escaped to the continent in December 1746 where he was warmly welcomed by Charles's father and given a pension, but Charles refused to meet with him in France and the two never met again. Murray died in Holland in 1760, aged sixty six.

O'SULLIVAN: John William O'Sullivan, leader of the Franco Irish officers who advised Charles and the man who is often wrongly blamed for the defeat at Culloden. His title of 'quartermaster general' may make him sound like a glorified store man now, but in the French army this was a highly prestigious office to hold. Given the irregular nature of the Jacobite army and the fragile relationships between the clans and the army's 'other' units, it's little wonder that history has somehow made him a handy scapegoat. There are some stories that, like the Comte de Lazuan who commanded James II's Irish army in 1690, the Irish officers attached to Charles were there to prolong the war and keep English/British regiments away from the continent rather than to win Charles's father's throne back. This would appear to have some truth in it as upon returning to France a hero, O'Sullivan was made Colonel of Clare's regiment of the French Irish brigade, indicating he had been rewarded for a job well done. A brave soldier, his only real mistake was not having the walled enclosures around the Culloden battlefield either ripped down or garrisoned.

DRUMMOSSIE MOOR: The bleak stretch of plain moor land, boggy and undulating in places, where the battle of Culloden was actually fought and where the clan graves and government burial pit are now situated. It wasn't the best of battlefield sites for the Jacobites by any stretch of the imagination, but they had little choice but to fight there.

ROBERT BRUCE: Crowned King of Scots in 1306 and despite great adversity, not just from England but from treacherous Scots, built up and trained an effective Scottish army that defeated the English under Edward II at Bannockburn in 1314, an English army that was three times their number. The awful film 'Braveheart' and a few narrow minded ill informed historians have questioned Bruce's integrity as he submitted to English dominance, like all the other Scottish nobles, at various points. He done this, as did the other Scots nobles, to keep his lands and title and the army raising potential that went with them, and let's face it, if someone holds a knife to your throat and says 'do you submit?' what would any sane person say?

King Robert also held the military ascendancy over the English in the years after Bannockburn, campaigning in Ireland and the north of England with relative impunity. Scotland herself has only ever had two truly good armies, one was King Robert's army, the other was the army of the mid seventeenth century who were veterans of the thirty years war in Europe, and ironically were instrumental in deciding the English civil war, siding with the English parliament.

A legend that Bruce promised the MacDonalds the place of honour on the right wing of Scottish armies after Bannockburn has persisted, and was obviously taken seriously at some point as there are records of them voluntarily yielding this position when they fought for Montrose in the 1640's. As for Culloden, it was the marsh in front of them that hampered their advance, rather than them being disgruntled about where they had been positioned.

MONTROSE: James Graham, Marquess of Montrose. Previously a Covenanter who opposed Charles I's religious reforms, Montrose was later authorised to create a royalist diversion in Scotland by Charles I, who was by now losing the English civil war thanks to the intervention of the powerful Scots army on the side of the English parliament. Montrose dully obliged and with two thousand Irish confederates under Alasdair Macolla, set about raising additional men for the King. Montrose achieved some great successes against his opponents while the main Scottish army was busy in England, but his force was poorly organised when not in combat, and perpetrated a few needless massacres. Their failure to take even the most basic military precautions like posting sentries led to them being surprised and routed by a portion of the main Scottish army under General Leslie at Philiphaugh, now returned from England in September 1645. Montrose himself escaped to Norway. He returned to Scotland in 1650 but the Argylist Scottish regime who had helped dethrone Charles I made sure he was betrayed and executed. Ironically, just after this, the Argylist regime switched to being Royalists and invited Charles II to become king of Scotland.

BROWN BESS: Affectionate nickname given by British troops to the land pattern Flintlock musket, which was in widespread use from the late seventeenth century until well beyond the Napoleonic wars, when the flintlock mechanism was replaced with the percussion cap firing system which was more reliable. The origins of the name 'brown bess' are unknown. It's been suggested that the weapon is named after Queen Elizabeth of England but there is absolutely no evidence to support this.

GRAPE SHOT: Anti personnel weapon whereby a cannon fired canisters or bags full of musket balls rather than a single solid iron shot, giving the cannon the effect of a giant shotgun. Devastating to infantry at close range.

COEHORN MORTAR: Short stubby artillery piece used for lobbing explosive projectiles at short range but also at a very high angle, ideal for short range bombardment or siege work. Deployed by Cumberland at Culloden for dropping shells just to the rear of his own men to 'encourage' them to stand and fight the Jacobites rather than run off in terror like they usually did.

RUTHVEN BARRACKS: During the eighteenth century after the 1715 Jacobite uprisings the British Government decided to tighten its grip on the Scottish Highlands by building four fortified barracks in strategic locations. Ruthven Barracks was one of them. The barracks was designed to house one hundred and twenty troops, split between two barrack blocks. In August 1745 some two hundred Jacobites tried to capture Ruthven Barracks. A force of just twelve British redcoats, commanded by a Sergeant Molloy, fought them off with the loss of just one man. By February 1746 Sergeant Molloy had been promoted to Lieutenant. He was still in charge when a larger force of Jacobites arrived, this time equipped with artillery. As a result the government garrison surrendered. Ruthven was where about three thousand men of the Jacobite army, including some fresh troops, assembled after the defeat at Culloden only to be told, in layman's terms 'go home for now', Prince Charles thanking them for their assistance. These three thousand men who included elite clan units who hadn't made it back in time for Culloden itself could, and should, have sought to obtain favourable surrender terms from Cumberland while they were still together and posing a threat, albeit without their cavalry, artillery, stores and figurehead. By dispersing they made the job of pacifying the highlands that little bit easier for the government.

The Jacobites set fire to the barracks and dispersed to try to evade the government forces who were now set on suppressing the Jacobites once and for all. The remains of the barracks today are pretty much how it was left by the departing Jacobites on 17th April 1746. Most of the exterior walls remain but little of the interior structure, flooring or roofing survives.

WOLFE'S: British regiments were named after their colonel at the time of the '45, and this particular colonel, James Wolfe, was to come to prominence in a different war in a far off land. At Culloden his regiment manned the enclosure that ran parallel to the Jacobite right wing, meaning that his men could subject the highlanders to devastating enfilade fire both when they attacked and when they retreated. Wolfe is one of the few Hanoverian officers to come out of Culloden with any real credit.

Surveying the battlefield long after the Jacobites had been routed, he spotted a wounded Jacobite soldier nearby, at the same time the unfortunate man was also spotted by General Hawley, commander of the Hanoverian cavalry, a man with a notorious reputation for brutality, and also the man the Jacobites had beaten at Falkirk. Hawley ordered Wolfe to 'pistol the rebel dog' but Wolfe refused, offering to resign his commission instead. Hawley backed down and eventually found a less scrupulous soldier to carry out this dastardly deed, a deed that was repeated across the moor. This deed was to serve Wolfe well when his men took Quebec from the French on September 13th 1759, as many of the troops who charged with him on the plains of Abraham outside the city were highland troops fighting for King George and carrying broadswords. Like so many great commanders, Wolfe was killed at the moment of his greatest triumph died at Quebec.

ORDER OF BATTLE:

Jacobite Army
(approximately 5,400 men)
Army Commander - **Prince Charles Edward Stuart**

FIRST LINE - **3,810 men**

Right Wing - **1,150 men** (Lord George Murray, brother of the Chief of Clan Murray)

Atholl brigade - **500 men** (William Murray Lord Nairn)

Clan Cameron Regiment - **400 men** (Cameron of Lochiel, *de facto* Chief of Clan Cameron)

Clan Stewart of Appin Regiment - **250 men** (Charles Stewart of Ardshiel, uncle to the Chief of Clan Stewart of Appin)

Centre - **1,760 men** (Lord John Drummond)

Frasers of Lovat Regiment - **400 men**)

Clan Chattan confederation Regiment - **350 men** (Alexander MacGillivray of Dunmaglass, Chief of Clan MacGillivray, for Lady Anne Farquharson MacIntosh, "Colonel Anne", wife of the Chief of Clan Mackintosh, Captain of the Clan Chattan Confederation and daughter of John Farquharson of Invercauld)

Clan Farquarson Regiment - **250 men** (James Farquharson of Balmoral, "Balmoral the Brave")

Clam MacLachlan & Clan MacLean Regiment - **290 men**

Clan MacLeod Unit - **120 men** (Malcolm MacLeod of Raasay) - attached to Clans MacLachlan & MacLean Regiment

Edinburgh Regiment - **200 men** (John Roy Stewart)

Clan Chisholm Regiment - **150 men** (Roderick Chisholm of Comar, son of the Chief of Clan Chisholm)

Left Wing - **900 men** (James Drummond, 3rd Duke of Perth, Chief of Clan Drummond)
MacDonald of Clanranald's regiment - **200 men** (Ranald MacDonald of Clan Ranald, "Young Clanranald", son of the Chief of Clan MacDonald of Clan Ranald)

Macdonald of Keppoch Regiment - **200 men** (Alexander MacDonnell of Keppoch, Chief of Clan MacDonnell of Keppoch)

MacDonnell of Glengarry's Regiment - **420 men** (Donald MacDonell of Lochgarry)

Clan Grant of Glenmorriston Unit - **80 men** (Alexander Grant of Corrimony) - attached to Clan MacDonnell of Glengarry Regiment

SECOND LINE - **1,190 men** (Lt.Col. Walter Stapleton)

Right to left

Clan Ogilvy Angus Regiment (Lord David Ogilvy, son of the Chief of Clan Ogilvy)

1st Clan Gordon Regiment (Lord Lewis Gordon, brother of the Chief of Clan Gordon)

2nd Clan Gordon Regiment (John Gordon of Glenbucket)

Duke of Perth's Regiment (Unknown)

Regiment Ecossaise Royal (Lord Louis Drummond)

Irish Brigade Regiment (Maj. Summan) (JACK CAMERON'S 'UNIT')

THIRD LINE - **400 men**

Kilmarnock's Regiment (William Boyd, 4th Earl of Kilmarnock, Chief of Clan Boyd) unhorsed
Pitsligo's Regiment (Alexander Baron Forbes of Pitsligo) unhorsed

Regiment Baggot's hussars (Unknown) unhorsed

Lord Elcho's Horse (David Wemyss Lord Elcho, son of the Chief of Clan Wemyss) unhorsed

Life Guards – Lord Elcho CAVALRY

FitzJames's Horse (Sir Jean McDonell) CAVALRY

ARTILLERY (Unknown)

2 x 2pdr cannon
3 x 4pdr cannon
3 x 6pdr cannon

Donald Cameron of Lochiel, *de facto* Chief of Clan Cameron, was wounded and had to be carried from the field;
Charles Fraser of Inverallachie was mortally wounded;
Alexander MacGillivray of Dunmaglass, Chief of Clan MacGillivray, was killed, with all but three officers of the Clan Chattan Regiment;
Lachlan MacLachlan of MacLachlan, Chief of Clan MacLachlan, was killed;
Charles MacLean of Drimnin was killed, with two of his sons;
James Drummond, 3rd Duke of Perth and Chief of Clan Drummond, was severely wounded - he was carried from the field, but died on his way to France;
Alexander MacDonell of Keppoch, Chief of Clan MacDonell of Keppoch, was killed.
Other persons of note on the Jacobite side to be killed at Culloden were:
William Drummond of Machany, 4th Viscount of Strathallan;
Robert Mercer of Aldie, an officer in the Atholl Highlanders Regiment;
Gillies Mhor MacBean of Dalmagerry, who led the MacBeans of the Clan Chattan Regiment.

More clans fought (and died) at Culloden than is apparent from this order of battle.

The Atholl Highlanders Regiment (also known as the Atholl Brigade) was mostly made up of members of Clan Murray, Clan Ferguson, Clan Stewart of Atholl, Clan Menzies, and Clan Robertson.

Also, the clan regiments are not quite as easily defined as their names suggest. Note that:

in the Clan Cameron Regiment there were also members of Clan MacFie and Clan MacMillan;

the Clan Stewart of Appin Regiment was not only made up of members of Clan Stewart of Appin, but also of Clan MacLaren, Clan MacColl, Clan MacInnes, Clan MacIntyre, and Clan Livingstone;

the Clan Chattan Regiment was mostly made up of Clan MacIntosh, Clan MacGillivray, and Clan MacBean, but also included members of Clan MacKinnon and Clan MacTavish, which were not part of the Clan Chattan Confederation;

the Clan MacDonnell of Keppoch Regiment included, apart from Clan MacDonnell of Keppoch, also Clan Macdonald of Glencoe (also known as Clan MacIan), Clan MacGregor, and Clan MacIver;

Lord Ogilvy's Angus Regiment consisted mainly of members of Clan Ogilvy and Clan Ramsay;

the Duke of Perth's Regiment consisted mainly of members of Clan Drummond;

Kilmarnock's Regiment consisted mainly of members of Clan Boyd;

Pitsligo's Regiment consisted mainly of members of Clan Forbes;

and Lord Elcho's Horse consisted mainly of members of Clan Wemyss.

British Government Army
Army Commander - '*William Duke of Cumberland*

FIRST LINE - **Earl of Abermarle**

Kerr's Dragoons (protected the left flank, led by Lord Mark Kerr chief of Clan Kerr).

Barrell's 4th (King's Own) Regiment of Foot (led by Lord Robert of Clan Kerr).

Munro's 37th regiment of foot. (led by Colonel Dejean) (after 1881 became part of the Royal Hampshire regiment).

Campbell's 21st foot, (led by 'Charles' chief of Clan Colville). (Today called the Royal Scots fusiliers)
Price's 14th regiment of foot (later the Prince of Wales' own.

Cholmondley's 34th regiment of foot. (after 1881 became part of the border regiment
).
The Royal Scots (led by Charles Cathcart of Clan Cathcart and James Sinclair of Clan Sinclair)

SECOND LINE - **Maj.Gen John Huske**

Sempill's 25th regiment, later the King's own Scottish borderers

Wolfe's 8th regiment of foot (later called later The King's Liverpool Regiment).

Bligh's 20th of foot (later called The Lancashire Fusiliers).

Conway's 48th foot (later the Northamptonshire regiment).

Fleming's 36th foot regiment

Howard's 3rd foot, later called 'the Buffs'

THIRD LINE - **General Maurdant**

Blakeneys regiment of foot, later renamed the Inniskilling fusiliers.

Battereau's 62nd (later disbanded)

Pulteney's 13th foot (later The Somerset Light Infantry).

Royal Artillery (led by Captain Cunningham of Clan Cunningham)
10 x 3pdr cannon
Clan Campbell's Argyle Militia (Col. Jack Campbell)

Cobham's Dragoons

Kingston's Regiment of Horse (later disbanded).

Of the British officers present, Lord Robert Kerr, was killed. Colonel Rich who served in Barrell's 4th Regiment of Foot lost his left hand and was badly cut on his head by a Jacobite swordsman, plus a small number of Captains and Lieutenants received wounds ranging from severe to minor.

Note 2: The majority of the casualties sustained by the British were borne by Barrell's 4th Regiment of Foot. Of the four hundred and thirty eight men present, seventeen were killed and one hundred and eight wounded, according to official figures anyway.

BIBLIOGRAPHY:

The '45: Bonnie Prince Charlie and the Untold Story of the Jacobite Rising
by Christopher Duffy.

The Scottish Jacobite Army 1745-46 (Elite)
by Stuart Reid and Gary Stephen Zaboly

The Bonnie Prince Charlie Country and the 1745 Jacobite Rising (Famous Personalities) (Paperback)
by James Aloysius Carruth

Robert the Bruce: A Life Chronicled
by Chris Brown

The White Cockade: And Other Jacobite Tales
by Stuart McHardy

Culloden
by John Prebble

The Wild Geese (Men-at-arms)
by Mark McLaughlin

The Battle of the Boyne: 1690
by Padraig Lenihan

Patrick Sarsfield and the Williamite War (History)
by Piers Wauchope

Playing the Scottish Card: Franco-Jacobite Invasion of 1708
by John S. Gibson

The Jacobite Movement in Scotland and in Exile, 1746-1759 (Studies in Modern History)
by Doron Zimmermann

Jacobite Threat: Rebellion and Conspiracy, 1688-1759 - England, Ireland, Scotland and France
by Bruce Lenman and John S. Gibson

The Jacobite Risings in Britain, 1689-1746
by Bruce Lenman

The Army, James II and the Glorious Revolution.
by J Childs

In the Irish Brigade
by G. A. Henty

History of the Irish Brigades in the Service of France from the Revolution in Great Britain and Ireland Under James II, to the Revolution in France Under Louis XVI
by John Cornelius O'Callaghan

Coming next in the 'Jack Cameron' series. A descendant of the Camerons finds himself in America as a former US cavalryman turned white scout for G.A Custer's seventh cavalry culminating in the 1876 little bighorn campaign.

"Greasy grass: Jack Cameron, the 7th cavalry and the battle of the Little Bighorn 1876"